Michel
Hope  he's
work. He spent 50 years not 30 in researching.

He was a great man, you don't have to believe, or you may. That's up to the reader, either way I know you will appreciate his talent in writing and the style in which he presents the story of Christ.

Mary & I are glad you are here, please make the mobil your home.

Richard Bastian
06:20:04

The Man Who Owned The Hogs

Leonard Dugger

Cypress House
Fort Bragg, California

The Man Who Owned The Hogs
Copyright © 1993 by Richard Bastian

All rights reserved. No portion of this book may be reproduced by any means, electronic or mechanical, without written permission from the publisher.

Published by
    Cypress House Press
    155 Cypress Street
    Fort Bragg, CA 95437

    Library of Congress Cataloging-in-Publication Data

Dugger, Leonard
  The man who owned the hogs / Leonard Dugger.
    p. cm.
  ISBN Number: 1-879384-18-3
  1. Bible. N.T. Mark—History of Biblical events—Fiction. 2. Jesus Christ—Fiction. I. Title.
PS3554.U3964M36   1993
813'.54—dc20   92-43933
                                                                           CIP

                First edition

           Printed on recycled paper

          Manufactured in the U.S.A.

Acknowledgments

My grandfather Leonard Dugger passed away before he could see *The Man Who Owned The Hogs*, which was his life's work, published. The final draft was left to John Fremont to edit, and I am grateful for his gentle care and skillful attention. Thanks as well to David Willis for his assistance. I am also deeply indebted to Richard Smoley for his critical eye and cogent introduction and Professor Gerald A. Larue for his penetrating analysis and thoughtful suggestions. In helping to bring my grandfather's dream to fruition, I accepted only those suggestions I thought he would have allowed. What errors remain in the text are my responsibility, while those sections that arrest you with their brilliance reflect the light that was Leonard Dugger.

May 15, 1993
Richard Bastian

Preface

by Richard Smoley

The Western world has been grappling with the meaning of the Gospels for over two thousand years now. For centuries they were taken—well, as "Gospel truth." With the coming of the Enlightenment, however, and a growing doubt about the supernatural, people began to wonder how much of these texts was history and how much was simply a fable to delude the credulous.

Two hundred years into this investigation, the results still leave something to be desired. We have had the changes rung upon the life of Jesus: besides the traditional view of him as the Son of God, he has been seen as any number of things: the exponent of a rational system of ethics (by Thomas Jefferson); a street-corner prophet of doom (by Albert Schweitzer); a magician (by Morton Smith); even "the greatest salesman of all time" (by Bruce Barton). Yet none of these views is quite convincing; the more exalted ones seem implausible, mythologized, while the debunkers leave us with a Christ that is too commonplace to have inspired anything, let alone the civilization that bears his name.

Leonard Dugger's engaging novel casts light on Christ from two disparate, contradictory, yet somehow fundamental points of view. For the unwashed, foul-breathed mobs that surround him and chant their hosannas, he is the object of blind, stupid, doglike faith. For the educated Roman Marcus Servilius and his even better-educated Greek friend Gestes Demias (whose name is a conflation of the traditional names of the two thieves on the cross), "Jeshu of Nazareth" is a pompous fraud, a demagogue, the erstwhile beneficiary of a flawed revolt. His miracles are a cheap confidence game; his profoundest wisdom has already been uttered (and uttered better) by philosophers before him; his subsequent deification is a narcotic for those too stupid or lazy to improve their lots on earth.

Gestes and Servilius, with their witty cynicism about "Jeshu" and the naivete and credulity of humankind, sound modern, too modern, it might first seem, to be entirely plausible; one could imagine them in a novel by Voltaire or a play by Shaw, perhaps but surely not in the ancient world? Yet Dugger's portrait of these men is surprisingly accurate, for the educated Greeks and Romans of the first century felt the same distaste for religion as we find in our own age. The ancient world knew little of the holy wars and doctrinal hairsplitting that the Abrahamic faiths, with their fervent certainties, have furnished in the two millennia since; polytheism is usually quite tolerant. Nonetheless, with its bloody sacrifices, its careless cruelty, its superstition and fear, Greco-Roman paganism gave plenty of reason for the rationalistic Lucretius, Gestes' favorite poet, to exclaim: *"Tantum religio potuit suadere malorum!"* ("So many evils did religion encourage!")

The ancients also saw through the human propensity to make God in man's own image: as the pre-Socratic philosopher Xenophanes (quoted by Gestes) pointed out, "If oxen and lions had hands, could paint and fashion images as men do, they would make the pictures and images of their gods in their own likeness; oxen would make them like oxen, lions like lions." Nor were the ancients fooled by the tendency to deify great figures of the past (like the Homeric heroes) or natural forces (like the winds and weather, or for that matter the sexual impulse).

All the same, as we've found in the centuries since, our faith—or our credulity—does not desert us so easily. For all the advances of modernity, we're still faced with two great impulses, which war in each of us as Gestes wars with Jeshu in this novel: the struggle between the desire to believe in something greater than ourselves and the equally powerful fear of being fooled. And often, as here, the struggle seems unresolvable in ordinary terms; our faith is crucified alongside our doubt. We can admit, again with Xenophanes, that "there never has been and never will be a man who has certain knowledge about the gods," yet something still pushes us toward the divine mystery. Can this contradiction be resolved?

To do so is perhaps an impossible undertaking, and I haven't answered this question so well for myself that I'm likely to answer it for anyone else. Yet one direction may lie in the tension that this novel articulates so successfully. Two hundred years of attempting to reconcile the "historical Jesus" with the "Christ of faith" has accomplished, as far as I can tell, practically nothing: we have no record of Christ apart from the Gospels, and what the Gospels offer is so contradictory and so unsettling that we can't rationally accept it. But perhaps this very impasse may offer us some insights.

What strikes me so forcibly about the various discussions of the life of Christ is that, while they often tell us little about Christ himself, they speak volumes about those who are doing the talking. The fanatic sees his own fanaticism; the rationalist sees delusion. The violent see a vengeful Jesus; the weak-willed see a flabby one. This mirror-like quality of the Gospels may not be a mere side-effect, but may lead us to the heart of their purpose. For I've come to think that these documents may be intended less to inform us about Jesus -whom, as we're learning, it's impossible to know in a historical sense—than to inform us about ourselves.

In recent years the Zen *koan* has entered the popular vocabulary, and people now commonly joke about "the sound of one hand clapping" or "your face before your parents were born." And we've also had some glimpse into the way *koans* work: by confusing the rational mind, they lead the seeker into an insight that cannot be articulated in rational terms, yet opens him up to higher wisdom. These days I find myself asking whether the authors of the Gospels didn't intend something similar. As Gestes so articulately stresses, Jesus speaks of peace, but has come to bring a sword; he exalts brotherly love, yet damns his enemies to hellfire.

I don't think we can resolve this contradiction in the ordinary way, by sorting out what Jesus "really" said from later accretions (as contemporary theologians are trying to do); the Jesus of the Gospels is both a contradiction and at the same time of a piece; take away something that bothers you, and the whole picture collapses upon itself. Take it all blindly, wholesale, and you may find yourself deluded.

Thus I think there is really no rational answer to the dilemma of Jesus—but it does not follow that there is no answer at all. An ancient esoteric teaching says that the four Gospels give different accounts because they are designed to speak to different levels of individuals, possibly to different levels of understanding in the same individual. Gestes would probably dismiss this as a rationalization in its own right, and so it may be. But I suspect the Gospels provoke the strange, contradictory reactions they do as a way of illuminating the contradictions in us. Any "answer" we may give to their riddle is merely an answer at a given level; if we go past it, we may learn more. Jesus would then be more than a savior or a fanatic or a wise teacher; he would be a reflection of our own being. And in this reflection the possible insights may well be infinite.

All the same, we have to consider our own historical situation. For you could also suppose that the myths of the Greek gods were designed with the same purpose: to confuse, stretch, and open the rational mind so that it could accept a higher form of knowledge. These myths eventually lost their power and were replaced by the more powerful myth of Christianity. Has Christianity, after two thousand years of its own evils and abuses, lost its numinosity in turn? It's possible; considering the state of religion today, it's even likely. If so, we will end up setting aside the Gospels as we've set aside the pagan gods and will have to encounter the ultimate mystery in a different form. But I suspect that the eternal struggle between doubt and faith, as exemplified in this novel, will remain with us. If we're clever, we may find a way of letting it lead us toward wisdom.

February 25, 1993
San Francisco, California

Table of Contents

	Preface	v
I.	*According to Marius Servilius*	5
II.	*The Ruse*	17
III.	*The Centurion*	40
IV.	*A God of Love*	43
V.	*The Book of Demias*	84
VI.	*The Miracle*	103
VII.	*Ironies*	112
VIII.	*The Possessed*	129
IX.	*The Making of a Mountebank*	132
X.	*Rogue's Harvest*	137
XI.	*The Widow's Mite*	144
XII.	*Disaster*	146
XIII.	*Lais*	151
XIV.	*The Search*	155
XV.	*In The Early Morning*	159
XVI.	*On The Jerusalem Road*	162
XVII.	*The Nemesis*	166

XVIII.	*The Greatest Lie Ever Told* *187*
	Afterword *191*
	References 193

The Man
Who Owned the Hogs

CHAPTER I

According to Marius Servilius

1

Yes, Caius, I was in Palestine at the time. I both saw and heard the man.

Since receiving your request, besides having refreshed my memory of those days by reviewing certain scrolls and miscellaneous parchments that I was fortunate enough to have salvaged from the demolition of the late fire, I have ransacked the Octavian and Palatine libraries and compiled numerous notes to supplement my recollections.

Furthermore, I have sought a medium whereby I can (entertainingly, I hope) tender the information you need before passing judgment upon the Roman populace for its enthusiasm over Nero's games. I have chosen to pen a story which, although primarily the history of a Greek polyglot, Gestes Demias by name, contains no little about this Jeshu of Nazareth as well.

You will bear in mind, of course, where direct conversations appear, that I make no pretense of being able to recall verbatim after these thirty-odd years. Striving only to keep in character and as close as may be to facts, wherein I do not quote or paraphrase documents, I recreate conversation for my narrative's sake. If in the process of this recreating, as is so seldom the case in actual discourse, I allow a speaker to complete his say unmolested by incessant and inane interruptions, I offer a two-fold excuse for so doing: I disremember such of these interruptions as undoubtedly occurred, and have no heart for originating others to approximate them.

2

When Corinth was destroyed by our legions under L. Mummius some two hundred years ago, a number of aristocratic, priestly, Achaean families, devotees of the cult of Hermes the Logos, resolved upon a voluntary exile until such time as Rome would permit the restoration of their beloved capital.

They selected the unsightly hills of Gergesa, on the eastern shores of the equally unsightly Sea of Galilee, as an ideal place in which to spend lives of perpetual protest.

Lest at sometime someone among them might forget he was residing in an alien land rather than adopting a new one, they engaged in raising swine, the one occupation which was calculated to be most repugnant to the pietistical Hebrew people about them.

For one century to the year, these Achaeans stayed by their resolve. Not until Corinth was rebuilt by Julius Caesar did any of them break their exile.

However, once this longed-for event transpired, with the exceptions of about four families, they lost no time in returning.

Gestes Demias, an only son, was the last issue among the few who remained.

He grew up in those hills under a most peculiar and, as it was to prove, a most formative combination of circumstances.

A naturally companionable, aggressive and Epicurean youth, he had forced upon him what, in many respects, proved to be a lonely, defensive, and poverty-blighted childhood. Neighboring children who would have otherwise found in him a rare favorite either avoided or plagued him due to the fanatical religious demands of their parents.

As if in compensation for a scarcity of other things, Gestes enjoyed exceptional educational advantages. Besides being the son of one who undoubtedly must have had a mind of remarkable penetrative and discriminative aptitudes, he was also the heir to numerous scrolls brought from Corinth by the exiles, chief among which were the three hundred books of Epicurus and the works of Democritus on Logic, Physics, Mathematics, Astronomy, Medicine, Poetry, Music, Grammar and Strategy.

As a youth he was encouraged to travel. He made two long and enlightening trips, one to the East for nine years, and the other to the West for four. While upon these journeys, he collected most of the religious data which were to so influence the remainder of his years.

Varied as are the rituals, insanities, indecencies, and inhumanities to be met with here in the City of Rome, it would surprise you to learn of what he saw within the myriad cults among which he strayed. Even a partial account of his experiences among the Lingam-Yoni sects of the Eastern world would have furnished Petronius the wherewithal to have added scrolls to The Satyricon.

All the time Gestes was away, his father was content to remain at home and herd swine, so long as he had ample time for studying his books. That he might later hand on to Gestes what he learned or reasoned out, he either bore his observations in mind or brought them together in manuscripts.

I still have some of his writings. There is at least one treatise which, upon your next visit to Rome, you will want to make it a point to read: "Concerning Self-Evident Truths." In it, to give a single example of its contents, the author makes this statement: "Of all such truths, I believe these two to be about the most impregnable: One, Zeno of Elea, in his classical mathematic paradoxes (Achilles and the Tortoise, the Arrow, etc.) absolutely disproves the possibility of motion; two, Zeno of Elea, in these same paradoxes, does not disprove the possibility of motion. The first is self-evident and irrefutably true from the standpoint of reason. The second is self-evident and irrefutably true from the standpoint of experience."

Yes, and there is another he wrote—possibly it is even the better of the two: "Concerning Philosophy as Narration," in which he states that most systematic philosophizing is merely a type of allegorical storytelling. The philosopher or narrator constructs a plot in which ideas, ideals, or "truths" play the various parts. If, in his dramatis personae, Idealism is made the hero, then Materialism is necessarily the villain. This theme is so worked out that Idealism triumphs, just as all proper heroes should. It will, I believe, greatly amuse you to see how cleverly he presents and how masterfully he substantiates this contention.

Gestes, while caring equally as much for learning, cared much more for other things than did his father. Although each in his particular way was a kind of Epicurean, whereas the older man found content in retirement and in the absence of pain, the younger, being of a more active nature, sought happiness or pleasure in companionship and accomplishments.

The son would undoubtedly have deserted for all time the Gergesan Hills directly upon the death of his noble sire had not something occurred across the Galilee just before he sustained the great loss that was to stay his departure.

Herod Antipas, the tetrarch, a man of luxuriant tastes, combing his ill-favored, sun-baked realm for a decent place in which to live, found as his best prospect a spot upon the west shore of the Galilee. The climate there, although well-nigh intolerable four months out of the year, is quite delightful the other eight. Moreover, on one side of the Galilee are the justly famous warm baths of Emmaus and, on the other, the remarkably fertile plain of Gennesar. Bringing colonnades and porticoes ready made from Rome, he had built, almost as if by magic, so quickly and proficiently was it done, a new city which, in the hope of profitably flattering the Emperor, he named Tiberias. It was a magnificent design admirably carried out, but, in common with just about everything else the Romans have done in Palestine, it was largely a failure by reason of its violating one or more of the countless prohibitions imposed upon the Jews by the Mosaic code. Wedged in between sea and mountain, to find room for it, the builders had to include within its walls the site of an ancient burial ground. For an Israelite to even walk over such ground means seven days of "impurity." As for living in such a place... The laws of Moses forbid! Herod tried to tempt his subjects by offering them free land upon which to build homes, but, aside from a few of the unorthodox... The laws of Moses forbid! As a final resort, the tetrarch was forced to people his new capital with immigrants from Persia, Egypt, Decapolis, Samaria, and Idumaea.

Here pork, unclean and forbidden to the circumcised, was openly cooked and sold in every hostel and caravansary throughout the city.

This suddenly put such a premium upon swine that Gestes greatly increased his already enormous herd. So prosperous did he become that he was soon able to hire Arabian youths into whose hands he almost completely entrusted his grunty fortune.

Thus freed from the necessity of doing manual labor, Gestes moved to Tiberias, there to devote his life to one of the rarest of all human endeavors—living.

3

At this time, I happened to be serving in the legion under a centurion named Marcus Numba and was stationed at a small, strategic village called Magdala, about an hour's walk up the seashore to the north of Herod's much fairer city.

To the boundless delectation of everyone in our camp, the Jews of that region, due in no inconsiderable measure to Numba's having espoused their religion and built for them a spacious tabernacle, were temporarily peaceful and obedient. We soldiers therefore had almost nothing to accomplish in the way of military duties.

Allowed to leave and stay away from camp almost at will, needless to say, we passed most of our time at inns, lupanars, baths, gymnasiums, cockpits, and other public houses in the more festive Tiberias.

Together with two of my camp companions, I was drinking at one of these inns one afternoon when five people, a Greek, a Jew and three Jewesses, entered and happened to seat themselves just across an aisle from our table.

Of the women, all of whom wore robes of a silk tissue which served only to display more advantageously almost everything they purported to conceal, two were well above the average of feminine fairness both in face and form, while the third was positively beautiful. They were just at that age when the fairest among the daughters of Zion are among the "fairest of all women." As is said of the Shulamite in the *Song of Songs:* "How fair and pleasant...for delights."

Thinking, or at least hoping, that possibly the five had

stopped there with the intent to recruit a man to even up the male side of their party, my comrades and I endeavored to make ourselves agreeably conspicuous.

When, for all our antics and overloud witticisms, we failed to so much as gain any obvious recognition of our existence—the group seemed wholly absorbed in a discussion between the two men—we soon became discouraged, and, except for an occasional glance at the women purely for the sake of the optic titillation, we very largely forgot about the newcomers.

During the course of our subsequent drinking, as is almost invariably the case sooner or later where two or more are gathered together in that godforsaken unholy land, our conversation turned to religion. In that unequaled desert desolation which is Palestine, what else is there to talk of except things "not of this earth"?

For my contribution to the discussion, I was telling, in a somewhat ribald manner, of a ceremony in which I once participated on the banks of the river Cydnus, when chancing to glance his way, I saw the Greek eying me with manifestly more than a passing interest.

Suspecting that, due to the presence of the Three Graces, he was taking offense at my anecdote, and noting he had all the earmarks of a much more competent opponent than I cared to needlessly antagonize, I so lowered my voice as to cancel all possibilities of his hearing the conclusion of my story.

Instead of allaying his concern, this precaution seemed to greatly heighten it. When my slightly inebriated listeners did me the honor of laughing uproariously on one or two occasions, he evinced a growing restlessness. He held a short conference with the other occupants at his table during which, they looked me up and down. This concluded, he arose and came over to where we sat.

"I ask your pardon for my intrusion," he began, "but I overheard the opening part of your little adventure on the Cydnus and would like very much to hear the rest. I am a rather gluttonous connoisseur of any and all varieties of theological evidence and am always anxious to add to my collection. We dropped in here on our way to my cottage, where we hope to amuse ourselves for the evening and would be ever so glad to include on our program your re-telling of this experience. I am one woman long among my guests; should you care to do so, and, if your friends will liberate you, I would like to have you join us and even things up. Gestes Demias is my name," he concluded.

"Marius Servilius is mine," I said, smothering my eagerness as best I could.

Upon my acceptance of his invitation, and, after bidding my friends a somewhat triumphant farewell, Gestes led me over to his table and introduced his companions: Azzie bar Jona, a contortionist and comedian of the tetrarch's court, a wholly pleasant, although rationally disgruntled individual of whom more later; Sarah bath Esau, Azzie's consort, also an entertainer at court; Deborah bath Daniel, my especial company for that and many another happy occasion thereafter; and the most comely of the three women, Gestes' mistress, a former *kadeshah* or consecrated courtesan whom he called "Lais" after the famous Greek hetaera of that name who was stoned to death in a Thessalian temple of Aphrodite by good women jealous of her pulchritude and of the evil life she led.

You should have known this woman, Caius; she would have altered your opinions of women.

I have yet to see another who could maintain such an enviable house on so small an income. Yes, or on any income, for that matter. Petronius and Tigellinus have staged more elaborate orgies under the auspices of Nero, but not once, not even in anticipations, have they ever known such congenial, such thoroughly enjoyable feast as we once did, thanks to the incredible genius as a hostess, of this Lais.

By the gods, Caius, I believe of late I have witnessed a score of times when, forced to attend one of his banquets and listen to Nero, abortional bastard of Parnassus that he is, plagiarize the odes of Pindar and Anacreon, I would have opened my veins out of sheer boredom had not a trivial detail in the table or else the food, more often by contrast than by comparison, caused me to live over again in memory some of the feasts we had in those far distant days.

4

If I still believed in them, I would say the gods of Olympus grew envious of that humble cottage in Tiberias, and, as a messenger of their ill will, sent to us in lieu of Mercury one of Gestes' Arabian swineherds.

Having finished eating one afternoon, we were still reclining about the table. Gestes, who was given to lengthy rationalizations, was elucidating an argument, the crux of which was this: having made the wrong choice between Democritus and Plato, it is doubtful that our civilization will remain extant long enough to ever make another such momentous mistake, another such tragic preference.

This discourse was suddenly terminated when the front door was flung open and in rushed an Arabian youth, who threw himself down at Gestes' feet like a terrified worshiper before the image of a supposedly hostile god. Out of breath and too afraid to speak, he writhed upon the floor and whined like a beaten cur.

Anxious and a bit impatient, Gestes alternately soothed and scolded the boy.

"Oh, Master, Master!" the swineherd eventually wailed, "a most awful calamity has come upon you. Your hogs are drowned in the Sea of Galilee, the whole two thousand of them. An evil magician, Jeshu of Nazareth, did this wicked and awful thing."

"Come, what are you trying to do?" asked Gestes in disbelief. "Who put you up to this mad prank?"

"It's true, Master; it's true!" sobbed the lad. "It happened while we were in camp having our lunch. Suddenly, we heard a great commotion among your hogs and ran to see what caused it. Alas, we got there too late to do any good. Every last one of them was drowned. I saw it with my own eyes."

The boy's sincerity was unquestionable. Gestes looked at him nonplused. He could neither doubt nor accept.

"But why did the Nazarene do it?" I managed to ask.

The lad started to answer but, looking back at Gestes, bit his words off so sharply his teeth clicked together. Tears began once more to roll down his cheeks. He stammered almost unintelligibly: "I don't know why he did it, except... Well, except..." He stopped helplessly, whimpered a moment, then in desperation, recommenced: "Honestly, Master, he claimed he ran the devils out of a madman and the devils asked leave to go into your swine and, once in them, caused them to run violently down a steep place and into the sea. I know you don't believe there are such things as devils and evil spirits, that you forbid us to be afraid of what you call non-existing bogies, but this was his only explanation. Truly, it was."

The silence that followed this information became painful, so painful the boy, unable to stand it any longer, soon broke it saying: "There were about eight or ten other men with the Nazarene, Master. They could have easily surprised your hogs and scared them over the cliff."

Silence again engulfed us, and again the lad tried to lift the spell: "At first, thinking these men must be demons out of Hell to have done such a wrong to a just man like you, we fled for our lives. But, then we went back with some men and tried to get something to repay you for your losses. But the Nazarene either had nothing with him, or by some magic trick kept us from finding it. We then tried to have the malefactors taken by the law and held until we could come and get you. But... Well, none of us had actually witnessed their evil doings and, since they all insisted devils did it, we were told: 'After all, you can't throw men in prison for what the devils do, lest we should all be in there.'"

Gestes gnashed his teeth. "The best we could do," the boy concluded, "was to chase them off, tell them to leave and never set foot on the hills of Gergesa again."

As Aristotle has wisely pointed out in his literary criticism, it is far easier for men to accept an impossible probability than a possible improbability. This thing was, to say the least, a possible improbability.

True enough, works of magic were only too commonplace in and about Tiberias. Exorcists, soothsayers, astrologers, fortune-tellers, dreamseers, conjurers; in short, mountebanks of every variety flocked there to live as parasites upon the illimitable superstitions of Herod and his court-favorites.

This differed from other anomalies in one noteworthy particular. Whereas miracles perpetuated upon human beings, rational creatures, are scarcely out of the ordinary anymore, this one was performed upon "dumb animals."

We were at a loss to account for it, and there was little if anything we could then do save to marvel and curse, it being already late twilight when we learned of this great work of the Nazarene's.

But, early the next morning—I spent the night at Gestes' house—we took a boat and rowed across the sea to Gergesa.

There we heard the Arabs' story verified by the other herdsmen and collected what additional information we could about this Jeshu.

We were conducted to the spot where the cataclysm had been enacted and saw the swelling corpses of the many swine.

It was a sorry sight. Vultures circled about the place in such numbers as to cast dark and loathsome shadows upon the surrounding hills. The bolder or hungrier of them even came down to alight upon nearby crags and upon distended carcasses.

CHAPTER II

The Ruse

1

Without predetermining just what we intended to do when we got there, we rowed back across the Galilee to Capernaum, a sprawl of limestone hovels shortly northeast of Magdala, where we had been told by the herdsmen this thaumaturgic destroyer claimed to live and to teach in a synagogue.

Our visit had been anticipated, and no one would admit to any knowledge of the Jew's whereabouts.

Some of the dullards were even brazen enough to pretend they couldn't understand anything Gestes said, despite his speaking their native Aramaic as well (I probably should say, on this occasion, at least as illiterately) as any among them.

Having intermingled with them all his life, Gestes knew these simpletons and their besetting weaknesses. In claiming to be God's chosen people, the Jews have made race prejudice a major tenant of their religion. Mindful of this, their varied superstitions, and above all, their horror of sacrilege, he resolved to gain his information through a ruse.

Stopping two fishermen recognizable by the odor they emitted, he asked, "This Jeshu of Nazareth, who is he anyway?"

One of the oafs, possibly hoping to scare us from our mission, said, "Some there are who claim he is the Messiah, the Savior, the..."

"What, another god!" interrupted Gestes a bit astonished.

With a roguish anticipation which almost made him forget his hogs, he continued, "But surely you do not mean to tell us, after all the saviors it has already had, this old world is still in need of being saved. Strike me dead if gods and sons-of-gods are not becoming more numerous these days than men and women! Before long one can gain immortality, at least in the memory of his fellow men, by the unheard-of act of admitting himself to be mortal."

"There is one and only one God, the Unnameable," said the Capernaumite with querulous dogmatism.

"Naturally," agreed Gestes, warming to the topic. "It is the vogue among gods these days. Since Alexander of Macedonia, with marked success, sought to bring the whole world under his sway, what is more to be expected than each upstart god should seek to do as much for the heavens? The Persians have had this idea for centuries, as you should know, seeing you Israelites stole it from them. For anyone not blinded by faith, it is easy to learn, from certain passages which later priests overlooked and failed to cull out when revamping the books of the Children's older prophets, your now-omnipotent God—by the way, his name, the sacred Tetragrammaton is ineffable, or as you put it, 'unnameable,' not because of its extreme holiness as your priests would affirm, but by reason of its not being a name at all but only a group of phallic letters so arranged as to form a single phallic symbol—was only a tribal deity of the Jews until, upon your being taken into Persian captivity, you remodeled Him on the order of the Universal Lord, Ahura Mazda. Alexander the Great, when he conquered Persia and spread her ignorance as well as her culture, gave Western gods this one-and-only notion. Since then there have been hundreds of one-and-onlys. It is most unfortunate. I have fears of its evil influence upon the arts. Think what a loss to Homer, Phidias, Zeuxis, and Praxitiles... Think what a loss to all Hellenic artists it would have been had they only Father Zeus for a model.

"But we won't go into that as there is another matter of far greater importance about which I would speak with you, or better still with your Messiah. Although I am a somewhat confirmed skeptic, there is one argument with which the religious shake my disbelief. They ask, for instance: 'If you found a beautiful palace out in a forest, could you satisfactorily explain its being there by chance, by Democritus' theory of falling diversified atoms, or by any other cause saving man built it?' Being fairly rational for a human being, I admit I cannot. 'So!' say the teleologists, 'and if you can't account for a mere building without a man to make it, how much less can you account for the man, a creator himself, without God, the supreme creator, to make him.' But, what they don't ask, and what baffles me is this: If I can't imagine a man without a god to make him, how am I going to imagine a god without a greater god to make him, or a still greater god to make that one? I follow this line of inquiry until my mind, rising from God to super- and myriad super-super-gods, gets so far out into the belittling immensities of 'the illimitable inane afar' I begin to have grave fears of losing it.

"All of which reminds me of the Greek mythmakers who, when asked what held up the world, said with complete assurance, 'Atlas.' When asked what Atlas stood on to hold up the world, they said with like assurance, 'a tortoise.' When asked what the tortoise stood on, seeing but not being willing to admit the futility of it all, they cried, 'Blasphemy!'—the final answer to all unanswerable theological inquiries.

"By claiming him the Messiah, you imply, I take it, that this Jeshu is the divine son of *Adonai*, the Author of all that exists. Where is this Jeshu? I would like very much to speak with him, to ask him a few questions. I want to know who engendered his father and who his father's father, ad infinitum?"

The fishermen were sullen and noncommunicative. But, after these questions, together with others of a like nature, had been repeated several times, one of the innocents finally relented and said, "I don't know who his father's father was, but Jeshu's father was Joseph of Nazareth, who, some say, was directly descended from King..."

"What?" interrupted Gestes with an eagerness which proved by this time he was talking more for the fun than for the supposed object of it, and probably, more for my benefit than for that of the fishermen, "do you mean to tell me your Messiah is the son of a man, a mere man? Come now, this won't do. Surely he was of some miraculous origin. Does he not know he cannot hope to compete with other immortals at this rate? Has he never heard the story of how Jupiter caused the night which he spent in bed with the beautiful Alcmene to last forty-eight hours, because in less time he could not have done justice to the making of the mighty Hercules? Has he not heard told by travelers from the East a meteor fell from heaven and begot Lao-Tzu, and his mother carried him in her womb for eighty-two years, which time he devoted to introspective meditations and to formulating his famous theory of life? The mother of divine Apis was impregnated by a stroke of lightning. What a thrill that must have been! Maia of Greece had bodily copulation with Zeus and bore Hermes the Logos? Undoubtedly your Messiah, as the mediator between *Adonai* and man, knows Isis of Egypt, being fecundated by her brother Osiris while still in her mother's womb, brought forth Horus, a golden calf. Why, any number of Grecian heroes were of divine conception. All the kings of Egypt and Babylonia were sons of gods. We have Nebuchadnezzar's own words: 'The god Marduk engendered me, and deposited himself the germ of life in the womb of my mother.'

"Blazing Gehenna, man, even a Nazarene ought to know he cannot be a Messiah and violate the ancient law of parthenogenesis.

"Why! To think I almost forgot to mention the fact! The unnameable himself, upon several occasions recorded in his own holy word, has added to the prestige of godly coxcombry or cuckoldry. He 'visited Hannah, so she conceived, and bore three sons and two daughters.'* He 'visited Sarah,' the wife of old Abraham, 'did unto Sarah as he had spoke,' and 'Sarah conceived and bore Abraham a son in his old age.' Yet again, he 'remembered Rachel, hearkened to her, and opened her womb.'

"A gay old God, I'd say; one I wouldn't mind mediating for myself. Which gets us back to your Messiah.

"If he is going to overlook this all-important matter of a divine progenitor, how is he, like hundreds of other deities, going to be born of a virgin mother? He simply must be born of a virgin mother! Take the case of Gautama as an example. He was nothing but a lowly, wandering, atheistic philosopher so long as he lived. Like Confucius, another skeptical philosopher deity of the orient, he taught that the immortals were, if not wholly pious fictions, so far removed from human actions as to make it absurd for men to fear or reverence them. But, some years after his death, one of his disciples proved to the complete satisfaction of the hundreds of his day and millions

---

*   Biblical quotations are referenced on page 193.

of the centuries since, that Buddha was sired by the Spirit of Truth and born of the Virgin Maha Maya. And presto! Change-o! Gautama, for all his disbelief, became a god, and so it was made that he left Paradise to come down to earth because, 'being filled with compassion for the sins and suffering of mankind, he volunteered, by his own humiliation, to expiate man's crimes and mitigate the punishment man must otherwise inevitably have undergone.' Which goes to prove your Jeshu is overlooking another vital element in his life's story. Think of the tender sentiment which would be lost to his worshipers did they not have a virgin to venerate, someone like Maha Maya, Myrrha, Isis, Maia, or Maritala. Then too, every cult must have a Yoni or Female Principle of one kind or another—at least they always have—just as you Jews once had the Ark of the Covenant, just as you still have the Holy Spirit.

"While he is about being born of a virgin, I might call Jeshu's attention to the fact it would be well for him, regardless of what it now is, to have his mother assume the age-old name for such favorites of the gods. Maya, Myrrha, Maia, mothers respectively of Buddha, Adonis, and Hermes, and, I might add another Maya, the mother of Xaca, and another Mais, mother of Mercury; all these are really the same compound names, just as many of the deities are compound beings, a combination of the male and female principles of phallic worship. Mare or Mar, in the Chaldee, signifies Lord, and Ri, the name of an Assyrian goddess, signifies the Celestial Mother. A union of the two, Mar-ri or Mary, gives us that androgynous deity so conspicuous in one stage of religious development. There's much more to it, but we won't go into the matter beyond the mere suggestion, or advice.

"Where is this Jeshu? I insist I must talk to him while he is still young and there is yet time for him to be born of a virgin. Where did you say I could find him?"

"I didn't tell you at all," mumbled one of the Capernaumites. "What is more, I am not going to. Besides, I didn't say he wasn't of divine origin, I..."

"Stand aside!" said Gestes with an exaggerated wave of his hands. "All my life I have wanted to witness a virgin birth, and I wouldn't be surprised a bit if this minute I am enjoying the fulfillment of that ambition."

"I didn't say that either," argued the fisherman angrily. "He has four brothers and two sisters, and, if I am not misinformed, two of them are older than he. In that case, how could he possibly have been born of a virgin?"

"No trouble at all," smiled Gestes. "When speaking of religious phenomena, always remember faith, that necromancy which makes the impossible commonplace. What can't one do by faith? Besides, it has been done before. Stories of him differ—were there ever stories of a god that didn't differ? At least one of them has it that before the Savior Krishna was born of the Virgin Devaka, she had conceived and born several mortal infants. The mother of Julius Caesar, being miraculously impregnated in a dream-affair with Apollo, lest a normal birth demolish her virginity, thereby robbing the future Emperor-God of an invaluable distinction, was delivered via an opening made by physicians through her abdominal and uterine walls. Incidentally, should one find it advisable to keep within reason, these physicians or men of medicine were profitably kept in mind; give them sufficient leave and incentive and they will work wonders. Just as in Rome, since Tiberius has imposed a tax on every Jew insistent upon remaining in the capital, and has designated the method whereby their identity can be ascertained, we find physicians restoring their foreskins to these unfortunates; Aurelius Cornelius Celsus, 'the Hippocrates of the Latins,' in his *De Medicina*, the greatest medical work produced by the Romans, devotes a whole chapter to methods of recovering the circumcised member. Just so in certain parts of India we find them restoring women their hymens, where such are more or less required of brides. They concoct injections and devise incisions so ingenious as to render a veteran prostitute more behymenated than a vestal virgin. They..."

"What do I care about your men of medicine? Men of the Devil they are," interrupted one of the Capernaumites.

"When it is a matter of being born of a virgin or getting herself a man, what does a Messiah or an Indian maiden care whether it is God or the Devil who comes to his or her assistance? They..."

"Just about as much," I broke in, "as a Jew cares when it comes to evading his taxes, or in any other way saving money."

"Right," agreed Gestes.

"But about your Jeshu," he continued, turning back to the other fishermen, "I just must see him about his divine conception, virgin birth, and such allied marvels. You see, I once wrote a book devoted to these very things. I'll admit having a probably unwarranted faith in the corrective potentialities of kaleidoscopic vista. I wrote it with the hope that in reading it, men would begin to compare their vital 'theologies' with certain outworn absurd 'mythologies,' and, seeing the interrelationship between the two, cease to be such deluded idiots. Knowing now this is too much to expect, I am willing to see my book unread, to forget the satire or ridicule I wasted in writing it, and offer it to the world for just what its title says: 'A Short Manual of Precedents Compiled for the Use of Mortals Desiring to Become Gods.'

"Regarding the place in which earthly deities should be born, it should always be the most humble possible as a sop to the meek and lowly who, after all, are the foundation stones of all religions; directly or indirectly it is they who pay the priests. Hermes, to name but one of a veritable host, was born in a cave. Horus, on the other hand, was born in a hovel. In order to appropriate the vast amount of symbols that has been woven about these two places, I suggest birth in a manger within a cave.

"There is also a choice and a preference in the date on which this Messiah should be born. Seeing there is already a day of universal rejoicing that is honored by Rome as the 'Birthday of the Unconquered Sun,' a day on which all public business is suspended, declarations of war and criminal executions are postponed, friends give presents to one another, and slaves are indulged with great liberties, I recommend December the twenty-fifth as the day of nativity. Mithra, the atoning savior of Persia, was born on the twenty-fifth. So were the old gods Bacchus and Osiris of Egypt, Adonis and Hercules of Greece, Chris Chaldae, and Gautama of India. Even the barbarians along the Danube cater to this precedent in the worship of Yule. in my book I give at great length astronomical reasons for the prevalence of this natal day.

"Because they happen somewhat infrequently, or at least once did, I believe there should be a display at the birth of a god. When Buddha was born, four angels came down from Heaven and held a golden net to receive him. Ten thousand worlds were flooded with light; the blind received their sight, the dumb their voices; the crippled became straight; the lame walked. Prison doors were thrown open, guards put to sleep; and court records of criminals were miraculously destroyed. The fires of all existing Hells were quenched and all the damned set free. Polluted streams were cleansed, celestial music filled the air, and peace on earth with a love of every man for his neighbor was proclaimed. I wouldn't advise your Jeshu to go quite so far as this. No, nor spread such gruesome tales as is related in the childhood stories of Aleides, Zoroaster, Yu, Salvahana, and sundry others.

"In a cave temple on the island of Elephanta is a most awe-inspiring bit of sculpture. It portrays a central blood-covered individual standing with drawn sword in the midst of a great multitude of slaughtered male infants. About him are the parents of the slain, supplicating for their children. The story behind this masterpiece of religious art is this: At the birth of Krishna, King Kamsa heard an angel's voice announcing that a rival ruler had been born in his kingdom. In order to destroy this babe, he ordered the killing of all newborn males throughout his realm. Alas, his efforts were in vain. Another angel warned the father and mother of the infant savior, and they fled with him into a far country.

"No, I wouldn't advise Jeshu to tell any such lies as these. Unfortunately for Messiahs, we have scribes these days who make note of the more outlandish caprices of either nature or kings. Their present silence might speak scrolls in future years. Some irreverent atheist might check up on these tales. Jeshu's believers, of course, would continue to believe just the same after this, but... Well, even religion should make some concession to fact. Or should it? On second thought, probably not. A less pretentious story will suffice. After all, a god is just another god, you know. A few shepherds might see a strange or extraordinarily conspicuous star appear in the heavens and, knowing thereby whatever god they happened to be expecting had arrived, go and find him. This was the case in the myths of Mithra, Yu, Julius Caesar, and others. For good measure, if the deity enjoys spectacle, and they generally do, throw in a few wise men and angels as in the stories of Confucius, Mithra, and Krishna.

"Can't you see how much these things add to the stature and dignity of a savior? I'm telling you, this Jeshu can't afford to remain in ignorance of such all-important considerations. He should have a copy of my 'manual.' No doubt I could sell him one. I believe I will. Where is he?"

The Capernaumites shifted fractiously, looked at each other for mutual encouragement and started to make their departure.

Gestes blocked their way, being determined to get as much satisfaction out of his ridicule as he could, since he already knew he could get nothing for his hogs. He assumed the air of a salesman and said, "Wait a minute. I see I have not convinced you of the merits of my fairly exhaustive, most instructive, and decidedly most appropriate book. Hear me further.

"My advice to would-be gods, and I base everything upon precedent, is that the less said about their boyhood, the better. A picture, statue, or effigy of the goddess Isis suckling the baby Horus, or one of Myrrha as she suckles the infant Adonis, inspires within us a devout worshipfulness. But a boy of seven or eight years makes a poor god, picture him as you will. After he has become a man, the candidate for deification will still have plenty of time to accomplish more than enough 'great works,' such as chasing people's hogs into the Sea of Galilee.

"Although I find them among the Egyptians, Babylonians, Assyrians, Aryans, Phoenicians, Persians, Greeks, Romans, and Celts, and have in my manual offered the names of over three hundred gods who did so, I for once go against overwhelming precedents despite the statement I made a few seconds ago to the contrary, and most urgently beg all contemporary and future immortals: 'Don't cause the blind to see, the lame to walk, the deaf to hear, and the dumb to talk; not if you expect to gain anything considerable by it. You will suffer too greatly in a comparison with certain mortals, men like Hippocrates and Herophilus, who not only effected cures themselves, but left us the formulae whereby we can effect them also. Then too, superhuman liar though you may be, I have my doubts any god or god-inspired scripture writer can surpass the tales told of the old Greek Aesculapius and his two daughters, Hygieia and Panacea. These early advocates of medicine worked cures so promiscuously and were even bringing the dead back to life in such numbers that Pluto complained to Father Zeus. It seems Hades was becoming depopulated. Aesculapius, who has since been born of the virgin Coronis and become a god himself, was once temporarily destroyed by a thunderbolt.

"One thing I treat in my book which I believe has not been used to its utmost in any religion with the possible exceptions of Zoroastrianism and Judaism—mark this well, for (as is becoming more and more evident), unless something happens to stem the tide, unless those few who have any intelligence begin to use what little they command, herein lies the limitless evil potentialities of supernaturalism. Wherever one finds religion, he finds a certain intolerance along with it. Yet in all Hellenic history, you will find few men who suffered solely because of their opinions. True, atheism was punished in Athens, but only by reason of its supposedly destroying the sanctity of civic oaths. Our omnivorous craving for gods, native and imported, mutually antagonistic and palpably absurd, resulted in two most beneficial effects: Next to having no gods at all, it is probably always best to have too many—it prevented the solidification of a dogmatic theology, and consequently minimized religious persecution. The common Greek could not admit such a thing as an impious or unworthy rite, believing as he did that any expressions of thanks and submission must be acceptable to whatever god or gods it might be addressed.

The Ruse

"Even Socrates, the too-often cited example of Grecian intolerance, was really killed, not as is sometimes averred, because he sought to win the youths of Athens to his unique philosophical or theological views, but, because he succeeded only too well in a passive role in indulging his sexual hunger, pederasty, or 'Socratic Love' and went from bad to worse until the authorities were themselves forced to force him to drink hemlock—reread Plato's *Symposium* and Aristophanes' *Clouds*. In the story of Rome, from the days of Romulus to the present, I find no censorship of ideas as such. Their gods are so numerous and so preposterous, we find Cicero publicly marveling that any two priests could pass on the streets without laughing at each other. Anywhere in the Roman Empire, excepting Palestine, a man can be as fantastically religious or atheistic as he pleases, so long as he does not employ his fanaticism as an instrument of faction, ambition, or suppression. Granted, you Jews were expelled from the Imperial Capital a few years back, but it was your insolence and not your theology which brought it about. A monotheistic precisionism would not allow you to accept or treat your betters as other than uncircumcised dogs, so Tiberius threw you out. Neither Confucianism nor Buddhism, probably the two most widely acclaimed of all religions—they are not religions in the main but systems of ethics—advocates or tolerates the coercing of converts or the punishing of nonconformists. But you children of Israel have ever waged wars upon and 'smitten' other nations for knowing better than to believe and behave as you do. Among you, murder for the faith's sake is not only lauded, but demanded. In Deuteronomy, you are told, 'If your brother, the son of your mother, or your son, or your daughter, or the wife of your bosom, or your friend entice you secretly saying, "Let us go and serve other gods—namely, the gods of the people which are round about"—you shall not consent, neither shall you spare, neither shall you conceal him. But you shall surely kill him, your hand shall be the first upon him to put him to death.'

"You have among you now a widespread cult called the Sicarii, or dagger bearers, who are bent upon killing off all Romans and friends of Romans, believing as they do they are committing murders for the Kingdom of God's sake. You would convert the world to Judaism by the gentle persuasion of promiscuous slaughter. I recommend this legacy of the Jews to future gods as a splendid method of making this life such a hell that men will think more about gaining paradise in the one hereafter. Am I not wise in this?"

"For once you are," maliciously conceded the older of the fishermen, "and in this connection, it might interest you to know Jeshu has said, 'Think not that I am come to send peace on earth; I come not to send peace but the sword. I am come to set man at variance against his father, the daughter against her mother, the daughter-in-law against the mother-in-law. A man's foes shall be they of his own household. If any man come to me and hate not his father and mother, wife and children, brothers and sisters, yes, and his own life also, he cannot be my disciple. Those mine enemies which would not that I should reign over them, bring hither, and slay them before me.' "

Gestes, as if scarcely able to credit his senses, looked to me for reassurance. All I could do was marvel: "The one who loves himself like that must be a god!"

"—or a lunatic," concluded Gestes.

Turning back to the Capernaumites he said, "You have in this Jeshu the makings of a great deity and a Son in whom your bloodthirsty, smiting *Adonai* should take a fatherly pride. He is on the right road. I must congratulate him. I will congratulate him! Where is he?"

The fishermen became sullen again.

"Anyway," said Gestes, "I'm with him. I always like to see a young and ambitious god get ahead in the world. So, even if you won't let me at him, you will at least convey my regards and give him the information I have given you.

"Yes, and lest I leave a good job uncompleted, you might tell him this also: Since all atoning saviors are born of the universal myth that man is by nature sinful and that the gods have a taste for the gore of their own sons, as hard on his person as it may be, he will have to submit to, or even bring about a sacrificial death. This, despite the philosophic scorn of Ovid: 'When you yourself are guilty, why should a victim die for you? What folly it is to expect salvation from the death of another.' The sacrifice of the innocent for the sins of the guilty; it is quite horrifyingly barbaric, quite contemptuously infantile. But take the barbaric and the infantile out of any religion of which I have heard and you would have very little if anything left. Besides, your messiah doesn't want to pay any attention to what these Latin poets say; they exercise the diabolical faculty of reason.

"Doubtlessly the most popular demise for mortals desiring to become gods is 'to cross over,' that is to be crucified. How old this precedent is, no one knows. I am told that, during his Persian conquest, Alexander the Great visited the cave temple of the Savior Krishna on the Island of Elephanta, and believing (correctly, I think) that he had discovered the source of much of Greek mythology, and knowing what value they would possess for his old master, Aristotle, had every picture, together with the inscriptions about them, faithfully copied and sent back to Athens. These pictures, as you can ascertain for yourself by consulting the works of the Stagirite, depict the life of Krishna from his miraculous conception and virgin birth, through his miracle-working career, to his death by crucifixion. The inscriptions are in a language which antedates the Sanskrit and is now totally unknown.

"Thulis, an Egyptian, was crucified some seventeen hundred years ago. In my manual, I give the histories of twenty-one crucified men and one crucified woman. Among these are such notables as Salivahana, Wittoba, and Sakia of the Hindus, Prometheus of Caucasus, Quirinus of Rome, Indra of Tibet, Attys of Phrygia, Serapis of Egypt, and Tammuz of Syria and Babylonia.

"Of this latter savior, Ctesias, author of *Persika*, wrote four centuries back:

> 'Trust, all you saints, our God restored,
> Trust you in our risen Lord!
> For the pains which Tammuz endured
> Our salvation he procured.'

"Blame me, not the poet, for this faulty rendition. Incidentally, many of the supposed prophetic references to a Jewish Messiah made by King David and the Prophets, when they speak of a Son of God, a Redeemer, or He who sits at the right hand of the Lord, are really references to this savior, Tammuz, and not to any Hebrew antitype.

"But I digress. Having been crucified, a savior should make it a point to resurrect himself from the dead after the manner of Zagreus, Osiris, Adonis, and their like. The vogue is quite universal: a dead savior should remain in the grave for three days, which represent the three months intervening between winter solstice and the vernal equinox, during which the sun (all saviors exemplify the sun, 'the Light of the World') is without its power, and consequently the earth is without its great lifegiver. Many, such as Krishna and Mithra, spent these three days in Hell among the damned. This is asking a great deal of an atoning savior, but like victims of algolagnia with whom I am inclined to suspect all atoners are closely akin, many seem to derive a weird satisfaction from such self-macerations. I leave this to the taste of the individual god.

"After a savior has returned from the dead, he should be seen, if not actually touched, before ascending like Fo of China, as the sacred writings about him put it, 'back to Paradise where he had previously existed for eternity.' A god can easily do this by casually threatening his disciples with the fires of Hell if they fail to see him walking about. And, if he is lucky enough to have a sculptor among his followers, he might follow the lead of Xamalxis of Thrace, who arranged to leave the impression of his feet in the solid rock from which he ascended.

"Thus in the lives of all saviors, despite minor individual differences, we have rehashed the age old story of the 'Unconquered Sun.' Born with the astronomical new year, he is killed at the spring equinox, and arises from the death of winter, thereby bringing salvation and summer to suffering mankind.

"This leaves for our consideration the best sources from which a savior can derive or, rather, originate a suitable doctrine. Here you can assist me. What, other than his having come 'not to send peace...but a sword,' does this Jeshu teach?"

The fishermen refused to answer. Gestes pressed them, and, at last growing angry, one of them squared his round shoulders and said, "You do not know what he teaches, and you will never know. For he has said to his disciples, 'Go not into the way of the Gentiles. It is given unto you to know the mysteries of the kingdom, but to them it is not given. For whosoever has, to him shall be given, and he shall have more abundance; but whosoever has not, from him shall be taken away even that he has. Therefore, I speak to them in parables;

because they seeing see not, and hearing they hear not, neither do they understand. I am not sent but unto the lost sheep of the house of Israel… It is not meet to take the children's bread and cast it to the dogs, and by 'dogs' he means you and all Gentiles like you."

"Which all goes to show he is a good Jew," said Gestes, "however contemptible he may be as a god. Does he have any more beautiful sayings?"

The other Capernaumite, younger and more intelligent, stepped in. Paraphrasing, or aping someone much more learned, he said, "He has. And you can search religions and philosophies the world over, and you will not find their equal. I can give you two of his sayings, which by their originality, their loftiness, and their universality, will of themselves declare Jeshu a man above all other men, a man divine, the true Messiah. Here they are: 'You shall love your neighbor as yourself,' and, 'All things whatsoever you would that men do to you, do you so to them.'"

Gestes blinked. A smile came into his eyes. "'Whatsoever men should do to you, do you so to them.' he echoed. "By the way friend," he hastened to ask, "Does this Jeshu by chance have any hogs around here anywhere?"

The fisherman wilted.

"Well, anyway… I'm afraid I can't agree with you on the merits of your Messiah's teachings," Gestes resumed. "In the first place, he stole them. As I happen to know, seeing it is one of my special abominations, he lifted 'Love your neighbor' word for word from Leviticus. The other he could have copied from many other sources. Confucius said some five hundred years ago, 'What you do not like when done to you, do not do to others.' And even if they were original, I still would guard my praise.

"True, as pure idealism—that is, as pure damned foolishness—they are quite commendable. But what is the merit of a mandament, even when promulgated with such solemnity and beauty of phrase, when both reason and experience not only fail to recommend it but absolutely condemn its usage? 'Love your neighbor as yourself'? Come now, be sensible; was there ever a more impractical and idiotic request? Is love so valueless as to be indulged so promiscuously? Must a neighbor make no effort to prove himself worthy of esteem but possess it regardless? Have those who are a source of pleasure or profit to us no greater claim to our regard than neighboring nuisances? Must we have no more love of self than we have love for willful beggars, murderers, ignoramuses, pimps, and catamites, yes, and hog-destroying Messiahs? It is useless to ask a man to love others as himself; he doesn't, he wouldn't, he couldn't, and he shouldn't! As a rule he loves his immediate family first, certain friends next, his townsmen only in a general sense, his countrymen still less, and, as for foreigners, they are mostly regarded as the somewhat menacing or ridiculous bearers of unpronounceable names. The tragedies of non-acquaintances touch a man but lightly. And so they should. Otherwise he would go through life in perpetual mourning. No, fortunately, we cannot measure up to this ideal, and it is stupid to ask us to even try. Does your Jeshu himself even believe or practice this thing? 'He that loves father or mother more than me is not worthy of me. Those mine enemies, which would not that I should reign over them, bring hither, and slay them before me.' The hypocrite!

"'Whatsoever you would that others should do to you, do you so...' Where is this silly Jeshu? I would like nothing better just now than to give at least one concrete example of where this ideal of his has led him into a grievous error."

To our almost complete surprise, the ruse at this point succeeded. Shocked out of what little reason he possessed by this final personal onslaught, the younger of the fishermen began to screech, "I don't believe it! I don't believe a word of it. I won't! I won't. It's all a lot of lies, filthy lies. Jeshu will tell you they are lies. He will call down divine fires from heaven to rot out your blasphemous tongue! He will..."

Gestes leaped forward and, grabbing the man by the throat, began to shake him ominously. "I lie, do I?" he yelled into the Capernaumite's purpling face. "So your damned Jeshu will tell me I lie? I have not lied, not once, neither have I misrepresented the facts, and I am prepared to prove it. Yet your Jeshu will tell me I lie? How do you know he will? Prove it! Prove it, I say, or I'll..."

I stepped in front of the other fisherman to keep him from interfering. Pointing as best he could to a nearby huddle of sodden shacks, Gestes' victim almost literally coughed up the information that the Nazarene was, "The-r-re."

2

Thus it was, Caius, that I came to see the man for the first time. We found him leaning upon a staff among a gathering of his followers. He looked up as we approached. There was nothing particularly impressive about the man unless you happened to remember he was a Hebrew prophet; in which case, you would have found him rather disappointingly human.

Having myself seen a number of his shaggy contemporaries, both prophets and rival messiahs, I could not but notice that his long sunburned hair, two locks of which hung down his cheek according to the law of Israel, was fairly well kept; his face and hands were moderately clean; and his robe of hodden gray was in a state of reasonable repair and cleanliness.

Otherwise, he was just another medium-sized, inconspicuous lout with an aquiline nose, dark skin, big mouth, and thick lips.

The older of our fishermen informants, probably intent upon diverting from himself any suspicion of treachery, stepped forward and hastened to declare the theological nature of our mission.

The Nazarene was immediately apprehensive. He looked straight into Gestes' eyes and asked: "What brings you here?"

Gestes came directly to the point: "I am the owner of some two thousand swine which you destroyed yesterday over in Gergesa, and I am here to learn how and for what reason you did it."

"What better reason is there than it should cause men to come unto me seeking to know my teachings?" asked Jeshu.

"Hypocrite," said Gestes. "Your fisherman friend there told us how anxious you are to make known your teachings. I'm no Israelite. I'm one of the 'dogs' to which it is not meet you should give the children's bread."

"The legions of Hell will no doubt be glad to hear you say as much," said Jeshu.

"'The Legions of Hell!' echoed Gestes in disgust. "You claim to be a superman, a divine light, and, yet you believe in ghosts, devils, demons, and evil spirits? It is upon such nonentities as these you would shift the blame for having chased my swine over a cliff into the sea? I expected some such lie. 'The Son of God!' You're an ignorant, meddlesome jackass, one that stands very much in need of just such a lesson as I intend to give you!"

Reaching out, he slapped the Nazarene resoundingly upon the jaw.

A groan issued from the rabble about us. Jeshu, however,

maintained his equilibrium upon his staff and offered his other cheek.

Gestes grunted his contempt: "You are hardheaded enough to stand up under it, are you? Try this!" He clenched his fist in preparation for a second blow.

Before he had time to carry out his intention, one of the Nazarene's disciples sprang forward with an uplifted sheep-crook and swung with all his might at Gestes' head.

I saw this move in time to jump in, and, with my sword, parry the blow which otherwise would have ended the story there and then. But, as if this fellow's attack were a prearranged signal, with nondescript weapons and savage yells, the rabble suddenly set upon us from all directions.

Fortunately, besides my sword, I had in my *cingulum militare* a long knife. Hastily handing this to Gestes, we turned our backs to each other and, as best we could, met the onslaught.

To our astonishment, we soon discovered we had a most helpful ally in none other than Jeshu himself. With his heavy prophet's staff he waded through his own supporters, clubbing them like rats. Since no one contested his assault, men fell to right and left of him as before a maddened bull.

"Desist, you fools of little faith," he cried. "Put up your weapons! Have I not taught you he who lives by the sword, dies by the sword?"

The mob gave way, but still glared its hatred. The Nazarene turned to confront us, possibly to see what effect his actions had produced.

"Don't fool yourself, Hercules," sneered Gestes. "It was not our lives you saved by your most valiant treachery. Moreover, it strikes me you are a bit inconsistent. I understood you came, 'not to send peace, but a sword.' You, like all…"

"Begone!" interrupted the Nazarene. "We will meet again, and then if..."

"We most assuredly will," cut in Gestes. "And," he added, determined to betray none of the glad relief he must undoubtedly have felt—for, to tell the truth, so greatly were we outnumbered that our ultimate victory was far from being a foregone conclusion—, "if this pack of curs still wants to commit suicide, bring it along with you!"

With a parting, contemptuous scowl at the rabble, he turned on his heels and walked away.

CHAPTER III

The Centurion

1

Although by no means reduced to destitution, with his swine gone, Gestes had no source of income. However, one arose, Phoenix-like as it were, from the very ashes or ruins of the other.

The day following its occurrence, I was telling some of my army companions of our encounter with the Galilean fishermen, when Marcus Numba chanced along just in time to overhear a comment I made pertaining to Gestes' prodigious knowledge of the world's religions.

He stopped to listen.

I saw my chance and took it. Aware that the Centurion, since his conversion to Judaism some months before by a Jewish interpreter, had become a puerile fanatic on the subject, and that he could not read Hebrew, Aramaic, or Greek, the only three languages in which the holy scrolls of Israel were available, I discontinued the story of our inglorious adventure and began a glowing eulogy of Gestes' linguistic and theological learning.

Numba was enthralled.

When I followed my lauding of the polyglot with a bitter denunciation of the society in which such a sage must work for a livelihood, a gleam came into the Centurion's eyes. The young interpreter who converted him had been employed in Numba's military transactions with the Jews, but to Numba's maddening regret he had lost this religious well-wisher at just the time he most felt in need of him.

Shortly after Numba entered upon that straight and narrow path which leads to a Jew's paradise, the true Messiah, for whose coming the Israelites had looked since they borrowed the mania from the teachings of Zoroaster, had actually arrived. He brought along an invincible sword, forged in heaven, with which to overthrow the Roman Empire and set up in its stead the Kingdom of the Jews. He demonstrated his messiahship, to the complete satisfaction of his disciples, by striking the river Jordan with his magic weapon and causing its waters to part as had the Red Sea before Moses. This done, he gathered about him an army and moved on Machaerus with intent to capture the tetrarch Herod Antipas. Built on a mountaintop some 350 feet above the Dead Sea, its walls more than 65 feet high, the castle of Machaerus is a formidable stronghold, even against a heaven-sent foe.

Herod refused to be taken. What is more, he asked the aid of Rome, and she, not being ready to welcome the millennium, sent out an army which met, captured, and decapitated this remarkable man, and all but annihilated his cohorts, among which numbered Numba's interpreter.

Thus his converter died before the Centurion had succeeded in committing to memory, or even to writing, the six hundred and thirteen prohibitions and injunctions of the Torah or Mosaic code, to say nothing of the one thousand five hundred and twenty-one things which the circumcised are forbidden to do on the Sabbath.

The prospect of finding someone who could help him transcend these difficulties delighted Numba. It gave him a new lease on life and promised him a mansion in Seventh Heaven.

2

That same afternoon I went to Tiberias to inform Gestes of Numba's desire to interview him.

On our way back to Magdala, I told Gestes of the Centurion's religion-inspired pangs, and I advised him as to the mask and role he had best assume for the pending consultation. I did not hear their conference, but deducing from the outcome that Gestes, acting upon his conviction that in order to masterfully portray the hypocrite one must have a part wholly contrary to his nature ("One cannot completely give the lie to a thing he only half disbelieves") must have played the hierophant in a convincing manner. At any rate, he won for himself a position with a fair salary as Numba's reader, interpreter, and spiritual advisor.

CHAPTER IV

A God of Love

1

In his manifold efforts to achieve sanity, Gestes was profoundly sober. However, he was almost inebriate in some of the madcap uses to which he put this sanity.

In observing learned men, he found a disdain on their part of nonchalance and rowdyism was one of the major obstacles to the popularization of knowledge.

Intelligence, being rare, is inclined to consider itself a freak, and so it acquires the most despicable characteristics of a freak. It idealizes its abnormality to the point of heralding it as the greatest of human attributes. It becomes uncompanionable, priggish, and, not infrequently, so arrogant as to bring about its own destruction.

Mindful of these things, in going about his self-appointed mission of freeing men from over-estimating their ideals, Gestes employed the principle that a man who brings his fellows to join him in laughter, regardless of how dynamic his doctrines may be, runs little risk of suffering martyrdom, and in the end stands a good chance of accomplishing more than the stately, somber-visaged pedagogue.

2

Two or three weeks after he began working for Numba, Gestes came into our camp one afternoon carrying under his arm a slab of stone which he had wrapped in his coat.

Noticing his rather futile efforts to keep from his face a roguish smile, I asked: "Well, what acroamatical monticulture has the illustrious bibliognost for us today?"

"I'll tell you. As a poet," he began, "I'm willing to acknowledge my inferiority to Virgil, Horace, or even Tibullus. But as a prophet, I concede no prestige to Jeremiah, Elijah, or even the Great Zoroaster."

With this announcement, he withdrew his coat to reveal a rude gravestone upon which he had scribbled this doggerel:

"Beneath this stone does Marcus Numba lie,
exclusive pupil of the great theologian, G. Demias.
If by it, he gained no worse than a Hebrew's Hell
Why, then in dying, he did wondrous well."

Underneath this, he had drawn the crude likeness of a cat playing with a mouse.

"If anyone present doubts a word of it," he commented, "then listen to this: Your most devout and filthy-clean minded Centurion, not knowing Hebrew, and making the mistake common to almost all converts to Judaism of thinking these so often dissolute books, the so-called holy writ of Israel, contains something conducive to a moral improvement and a spiritual uplift, has assigned me the pleasant task of translating such passages from them as I see fit; the which, he is going to consume for his soul's sake. Poor soul! I started to work this afternoon, and would like you to listen to what I have accomplished.

"In the book called Qoheleth,* I find this: 'For that which befalls the sons of man befalls beasts; even one thing befalls them: as the one dies, so dies the other: yes, they all have one breath; so that a man has no preeminence above a beast; for all is vanity. All go unto one place; all are of the dust, and all turn to dust again. All things come alike to all: there is one event to the righteous and to the wicked, to the good and the clean and to the unclean; to him that does and to him that does not make sacrifices: as is the good, so is the sinner; ...For to him that is joined to all the living there is hope: for a living dog is better than a dead lion. For the living know they shall die: but the dead know not anything, neither have they any more a reward; for the memory of them is forgotten. Also their love and their hatred and their envy is now perished; neither have they any more a portion for ever in any thing that is done under the sun... Whatsoever your hand finds to do, do it with all your might: for there is no work, nor device, nor knowledge, nor wisdom in the grave, where you go.'

"Can't you picture Numba's immortal soul feasting upon these bits of divinely inspired Pyrrhonism?

"In Deuteronomy: 'You shall not eat of any thing that dies of itself: you shall give it unto the stranger that is in your gates, that he may eat it; or you may sell it unto an alien; for you are a holy people.'

"No doubt we have in this verse the basis for certain commercial practices which characterize God's chosen people."

"Yes," said a young legionnaire, "and no doubt therein lies the explanation for the peculiar taste of some of the meat Numba has carted out here for us 'heathens' to eat."

---

*   Ecclesiastes

"I wouldn't be at all surprised," conceded Gestes. "The Jews tell me a conversion to Judaism works a profound change in one's morals. I'd keep an eye on the Centurion now he is one of the Chosen.

"But, to get back to this holy writ: I have culled these morsels from various books and will prune some of excess verbiage: 'And, God spoke unto Moses saying: Vex the Midianites and smite them. The angel of God went out and smote the camp of the Assyrians a hundred fourscore and five thousand. When your God has delivered it (the city) into your hands, you shall smite every male thereof with the edge of your sword; but the women (now, that's different), and the cattle, and all that is in the city, you shall take unto yourself. When you go forth to war against your enemies, and your God has delivered them into your hands, and you have taken them captive, and see among the captives a beautiful woman, and have a desire for her (how delicately put), bring her home. Go into her (not so delicately put). If you have no delight in her, then let her go.'

"To think these righteous rapists should find in the night life of old father Zeus and the tipsiness of Bacchus the wherewithal to be greatly scandalized. As if seducing virgins and getting hilarious on good wines were not almost infinitely less undesirable than the eternal smiting of your neighbors because of their refusal to subscribe to your superstitions.

"In Numbers (I prune here also), 'They warred against the Medianites, (smote them) as God commanded Moses, and they slew all the males. The children of Israel took all the women of Median captives. Moses said unto them: Kill every woman that has known a man by lying with him. But all the women that have not known a man by lying with him, keep alive for yourselves.'

"If the gods of Rome encouraged this type of thing, within

ten years her legions would be crying, like Alexander the Great, for new women to conquer. But all in vain! Greece, Palestine, and all other foreign nations would be alive, thereafter, only in a Roman's memory of bed-er days.

"In Genesis: And she (Rachel, the barren wife of Jacob) said: 'Behold my maid Bilhah; go in unto her; and she shall bear upon my knees, that I may also have children by her. And she gave him Bilhah her handmaid to wife; and Jacob went in unto her.'

"This same situation, wherein the barren wife offers her beautiful handmaid to a willing husband, happens more than once in these holy Scriptures. No wonder we have reactionary religionists yearning for a return of the 'days of old' and the 'staunch' morality then in vogue.

" 'David sent messengers, and took her: (Bathsheba, wife of the Hittite, Uriah) and she came in unto him and he lay with her.' What a typical Scriptural lie! What a characteristic 'man of God!' No mention or evidence whatsoever of any consideration for the woman, no seduction, no romance. No thought of the husband. No regard for common decency. No element of color. Just the brutal gratification of lust. 'David sent messengers, and took her,…and lay with her.'

"But it begins to appear in subsequent passages that even David isn't going to get away with his adultery with Bathsheba and the murder of her noble husband. This is too heinous for even the God of Israel: 'Said Yahweh,' in II Samuel, 'Behold, I will raise up evil against you (David) out of your own house, and I will take your wives before your own eyes and give them unto your neighbor, and he shall lie with your wives in the sight of this sun. For you did it secretly, but I will do this thing before all Israel.'

"Bravo! Bravo! Heavenly atonement… The innocent wives

to suffer for the transgressions of the wicked husband. A perfect example of what I call...

Divine Injustice

'David,
For the wrongs you did Uriah,
By Myself, I swear to Hell,
I will so maltreat your women
It will injure you as well.'

"Pardon the lyrical outburst; excessive admiration forced it upon me.

"I hope you fellows will not make the mistake of believing me the victim of a sudden and acute attack of squeamishness; it is just that (mindful of the supposed divine authorship, exemplary rectitude, and archetypical nicety of this collection of pointless sex myths) I can hardly pick the damned books up without succumbing to a generalized pugnacious aversion.

"I also hope I am not corrupting the morals of any of His Imperial Majesty's little soldiers by reading holy writ aloud."

"What of it?" laughed an old veteran. "Go right ahead. I'm surprised to learn these accursed heavenly-minded Jews had such interesting writers. It's educational. If you run across one of those after-the-war-is-over stories, translate it and save me a copy."

"That I shall," said Gestes.

"And," said another, "if you will do the copying, I'll furnish the parchment and sell this holy writ to the soldiers. We'll go fifty-fifty on the returns."

"You should have never joined the army," laughed Gestes. "You were born to be a merchant."

"What does Numba say?" I asked him.

"He assures me that his Yahweh is, like Cupid, a god of love. From the quotations I have just provided, you can easily see that he is, after a manner.

"In fact, omitting his jealousy of other gods, his incessant smiting of non-believers in Himself, and his pertinacious solicitations for meat and grain with which to glut his priests, I would say these sacred lucubrations show affairs of love to be his primary interest. He visited several of his female votaries, Hannah—Leah, Sarah, and Rachel are prominent—and 'opened' their wombs. They then 'conceived and bore.' On the other hand, being angry with them, he 'entirely closed the wombs of all in Abimelech's household. He ruled out those male devotees whose damaged sexual organs disqualified them for acquitting themselves honorably in his rites: 'He that is wounded in the stones, or has his privy member cut off, shall not enter into the congregation of God. Anyone with 'broken testicles' may not be his priest. A devotee who willfully destroys his generative powers is twice a murderer. And the unfortunate one who is born impotent may not participate in his worship.

"It is also written: 'When two men are fighting with one another, if the wife of one of them comes to the rescue of her husband and puts out her hand to seize his assailant by the private part, you shall cut off her hand, and you shall have no pity on her.' An animal sexually injured is not acceptable to him as a sacrifice. His chosen may not geld any of his creatures for table use or for marketing. They may not even have an accursed Gentile perform the operation upon their beasts.

"Nor are potentialities sufficient. The first of his commandments found in these holy books is 'Be fruitful and multiply and replenish the earth.' None of his followers may abstain from sexual indulgence, not even for the sake of the Law. The one who would devote his life to incessant religious study and practices must first marry and have children, a boy and a girl. Only after that may he withdraw from the world and worldly things, leave his wife and children, and devote all his waking hours to studying the Torah.

"Masturbation is an abomination to Yahweh and *coitus interruptus* is a deadly sin. He murdered Onan because, despite his aversion to such practices, when he commanded Onan to lay with his brother's widow, Onan withdrew and spilled his 'seed on the ground.'

"If one of his fair devotees dies virginal, may alien gods help her, for he won't. Take a case found in Judges: Jephthah's silly oath resulted in his daughter's being condemned to die. She accepted her fate, asking only one favor: 'Let me alone for two months, that I may go up and down the mountains and bewail my virginity…'

"For a Jewess to live without bearing children; that is, without doing her foremost religious duty, is even worse than to die a virgin. To escape a life of barrenness, A Jewess will resort to deceit, treachery, or most any other crime and feel the end justifies the means. As did Rachel, Sarah, because God had 'restrained' her from bearing, asked her husband to 'go in unto' her maid that she might 'obtain children by her.' Tamar deceived her father-in-law, made him believe her a *kadeshah*, or sacred prostitute, in order to be fecundated by him. Because in their secluded retreat there was not another man 'to come in unto' them 'after the manner of all the earth,' Lot's two daughters, got their old dad drunk on wine and seduced him.

"Throughout every one of these divinely inspired works, we find a special regard paid the powers of generation. When Yahweh made a covenant with Abraham wherein he agreed to take the Jews as the chosen people, the pact was consummated in the most binding way he could think of: in blood of the phallus, creator and symbol of the Creator, source of human life and of all that exists. 'This is my covenant which you shall keep, between me and you and your seed after you: Every male among you shall be circumcised. You shall circumcise the flesh of your foreskin; and it shall be a token of the covenant between me and you... And the uncircumcised manchild whose flesh of his foreskin is not circumcised, that soul shall be cut off from his people; he has broken my covenant.'

"In these books, when the occasion arises for one to take an especially momentous oath, he has to put his hand upon the most sacred object available. The Chosen place their hands upon, or rather 'under' their members. Old Abraham, seeing his days were drawing to a close, and, wanting to make it imperative to the elder in his household, that his son Isaac take a wife, not from among the fair ones of Canaan, but from among Abraham's own people, called Eliezer to him and said: 'Put, I pray you, your hand under my penis, and I will make you swear by Yahweh, the God of Heaven and the God of the earth...' A situation of like importance presenting itself to him, Jacob swore Joseph in the same manner.

"This deity's favorite manifestation is in the form of a pillar, foremost among phallic emblems. For example: 'It came to pass, as Moses entered into the tabernacle, a cloudy pillar descended and stood at the door of the tabernacle, and God talked with Moses... All the people who saw the cloudy pillar...rose up and worshiped. As the children fled from Egypt, 'Yahweh went before them by day in a pillar of a cloud, to lead them the way; and by night in a pillar of fire, to give them light.'

"Not only does he assume the form of a pillar himself, but his priests and prophets set up pillars 'for a sign and a witness unto him.' Jacob, placing one 'at the border' of Egypt, gave this quoted reason for so doing. Elsewhere Jacob raised up another, of which he said: 'This stone, which I have set up for a pillar, shall be God's house.' (Phallic deities are frequently believed to reside in stone phalli.) Jacob 'poured a drink-offering thereon, and he poured oil thereon,' which is the universal method of anointing the phallus when making offerings to it as emblematic of the Creator.

"In these works, his own dictated books, we find him repeatedly declared a lingam and addressed as one. Moses called him 'the rock that begot you,' and David, besides calling him 'the Rock of Israel,' admonishes the Chosen in this way: 'O come, let us sing unto God: let us make a joyful noise to the rock of our salvation.' After he had 'visited Hannah, so she conceived and bore three daughters,' we find her exclaiming: 'There is none holy like Yahweh... neither is there any rock like our God.'

"These selections constitute but a bare smattering of the evidence these scrolls contain which attest to the fact this 'Rock of Israel' was an undisguised representation of virility until the chosen people were taken into Babylonian captivity and found out how poorly Yahweh compared to Ahura Mazda. Thereafter, he was invested with the spirituality of which his children are now so redundantly proud.

"Yet today, the worshipers of this only-slightly disguised 'Lord of the Opening' are horrified by the frankness of the Hindu proverbs: 'The seat of a woman's religion is in her pudendum. Men worship not with their hearts but with their genitalia.'

"I have at my cottage in Tiberias a manuscript entitled, 'Concerning Religio-Sexual Phenomena.' A rabbi, whom I once allowed to read it, waxed so enthusiastic he acclaimed this book 'the world's foremost masterpiece of sacrilege.' Without claiming for it any such inordinate merit, I still believe I can recommend this work to you fellows as one containing much you would like to review. In it I endeavored to amass such an overwhelming bulk of evidence as would force the general acceptance of numerous conclusions. I was younger when I executed these designs, and had yet to learn that superstition and prejudice are harder and less malleable than adamant.

"I will not take time to elaborate my conclusion that countless elements of the god-idea were born of sex and have ever since been conditioned by man's sexual knowledge.

"As to point of time, the genesis of phallic worship is no doubt irretrievably lost. On that score, all we can say with certainty is this: Every people of past centuries who has left enduring records of its existence has also left unmistakable evidence of its Priapean faith. But, as to the genesis of this particular form of devotion, I have brought together in my book considerably more than I will trouble you fellows to hear.

"Who would argue that sexual congress, besides being the first cause of our being brought into the world, furnishes us one of our keenest pleasures, one of our greatest rewards for staying here. So intense is the enjoyment thus afforded, not uncommonly one feels it somehow transcends the earthly, human, and natural; it smacks of the heavenly, divine, and supernatural. Thus we find religious emotions springing from sexual emotions. Through these sex-born religious emotions, we find men deifying the source of their ecstasies and holding that God is love. Since to ape God, flatter him, grovel before him, and wheedle his favor universally constitute the chief passions of religionists, we find them devotedly copulating. Or writing lengthy theological treatises, divinely inspired scriptures, promulgating the doctrine that in coitus, the immortalizing act of God, one tastes the Divine Essence and is momentarily absorbed into the Divine Soul. Or setting up stones for signs and for witness unto the phallus, the Creator, the 'Giver of Life'; and pouring drink-offerings thereon, and pouring oil thereon; and thereby hoping, yes, even expecting to get blessed with more beautiful woman, larger members, greater virility, and countless other heaven-sent boons.

"As incredible as it now seems, there was a time when we, the self-styled civilized races, like those we now call 'savages,' believed women to be the sole progenitors. All the deities of that time were of the female gender; all cosmogonies spoke of the Celestial Mother. Since the origin of everything they could observe was either born or hatched from eggs, they made the common human error of taking it for granted that all other things, the world included, originated the same way.

"We will probably never learn who the first of these goddesses was, but stories of a black virgin permeate the most ancient of all religious legends that have come down to us. Such a one was worshiped among the Ethiopian or early Cushite race, the very people who some say carried civilization to Egypt, India, and Chaldea. This black virgin might be the original Queen of Heaven, the Yoni of Yonis, the Mother of all the Gods. Such a concession, however, would be considered the ultimate in blasphemy by certain Egyptians, worshipers of the Virgin Neith. Her very name means, 'I come from myself.' She says, through the medium of an engraving on her temple at Sais: 'I am all that was and is to be.' Yes, and to the Hindu devotees of Oma-Oma as well, for they claim their goddess existed not only before any of the other deities but before existence itself. We find a most curious and tell-tale fossil of the female Creator in Genesis, first of the holy books of Israel: 'And the earth was without form and void; and darkness was upon the face of the deep. The *ruach* moved upon the face of the waters.' *Ruach*, a feminine noun, means 'the spirit of god.'

"Probably because of the existence of eunuchs, man made his greatest discovery of all time: he played a part in the begetting of children. Thereafter, he began to make his influence felt in various noteworthy ways. Lineage began to be traced through the father, where before it had been traced only through the mother. Polyandry, possibly the universal marital custom at that time—it still is among savages in this stage of sex-knowledge—gave way to polygamy and monogamy. Deities began to change their gender. However, although wanting to assert male preeminence over the female principle, these early theologians, in trying to name one god as 'the first to exist,' could not, in view of the obvious part women play in childbirth, make this first among the gods wholly masculine, and so made it androgynous. One of the Hindu's sacred books says: 'The Supreme Spirit in the act of creation became twofold; the right side was male, the left side female.'

"Incidentally, in the Hebrew Scriptures, fathers refer to their sons as the children of their right side. You are acquainted with the superstition back of this: boys are made by the right and girls by the left testicle. It is altogether possible you have run across an instance where a man, being adverse to the advent of other daughters into his house, ties a cord securely about his left stone every time he 'goes in unto' his wife, or has had the left one removed entirely. It is a venerable fallacy and, as is so often the case with traditional ignorance, the mere facts that it doesn't work and is quite painful besides, have never prevailed against it.

"Anyway, so it is we find the god of the *Bhagavad-Gita*, a sacred Hindu work written some two thousand years ago, says, 'I am the father and mother of the world.' The Creator is often symbolized by the image of some hermaphroditic insect, such as the snail, which, endowed with the organs of both sexes, can copulate with another of its kind reciprocally. Many of the gods bear names of the Lingam-Yoni composition. In the Hebrew Scriptures, the 'Rock of Israel' is called *Eliohim,* plural in form and construction, from El, the male, and Oh, the female essence.

"In Genesis there are numerous passages which point to the dual sexuality of the 'One and Only God'. *Elohim* said, 'Let us make man in our likeness...' So *Elohim* created man in his own image. 'In the day that *Elohim* created man, in the likeness of *Elohim* created he him; male and female created he them; and blessed them, called their name Adam...' And *Elohim* said, 'Behold, the man is become as one of us.'

"There lives in Alexandria a Jewish philosopher named Philo, a very learned nonsensical fellow, who, agreeing Adam was an androgyne 'in the likeness of *Elohim,*' goes on to say: '*Elohim* separated Adam into his sexual component parts, one male, the other female, Eve, taken from his side. The longing for reunion which love inspired in the divided halves of the originally dual being is the source of sexual pleasures, which is the beginning of all transgressions.'

"Although I have little but contempt for his theories of love and 'original sin,' I am mindful of the fact that the most ancient of human records preserve vague accounts of devastating religious wars waged between the Yonites and the Lingamites. The fundamental issue of these wars, whose gods are the true gods and whose the false, has never been settled and still is with us. So we will have to agree that there is some truth in Philo's referring to what we may call the first divorcement as 'the beginning of all transgressions.'

"Incidentally, in this connection it might interest you to know that, according to a Chaldean legend, when the two elements of their deity separated, the female, in order to avoid entering into an incestuous relationship with her persistent male element, transformed herself into an animal. But the god, seeing what she had done, made it serve his own purpose. He secretly made himself a male of the same species and, as such, was welcomed by the goddess. When, too late, she discovered who he really was, she transformed herself into another animal. He continued to catch on and deceive her until, so the story goes, the world was populated with its many and varied species, men, animals, fowls, reptiles, insects and fishes."

"By the gods," marveled one of the soldiers. "It sounds silly, and yet I've never heard the thing accounted for in a better way."

"If," admitted Gestes, "without knowing anything about them, and without going to the trouble of learning anything about them, we nonetheless must account for such things, I suppose this Chaldean tale is as good as any."

"You win," amiably shrugged the legionnaire. "Go right ahead as if I had never interrupted to show my ignorance."

"Then," smiled Gestes, "to return to my conclusion: in that we find religious groups the world over and from remotest antiquity in which these excesses have occurred, not alone in those of a particular paradigm, but in the most varied of cults, we must accept the presence in religion of a considerable sexual admixture. I need dwell upon this proposition no further than to remind you of the religious festivals, the names of which, Bacchanalia, Dionysiaca, Priapeia, Saturnalia, Lupercalia, Hilaria, and the like, and, more especially the many words derived from these names have so enlarged and enriched the erotikon's vocabulary.

"In those mystical experiences in which the devotee enters into a supposed union with the divine and thereby thinks to offer a personal testimony to the inerracy of his creed, in actuality, he but experiences a mistaken sex-ecstasy. That in those so-familiar religious festivals in which the transfer of devotional rapture into sexual sensation is especially evident, in which worshipful frenzies culminate in erotic orgies, the sexual is a continuation and heightening of the religious; basically, the legitimate physical outlet for a presumedly purely devotional urge.

"The worship of Dionysus proffers us a good example of the interchangeability of religious and sexual ardor. In observing the Dionysiaca, the devout seek to attain a state of ecstasy, since only in this way can he or she enter into communion with the deity. I hasten to add that with some few, those rare human beings whom even religion cannot make barbaric loons, this is quite a dignified affair. But the vast majority, like the Psalmist, want to 'sing unto' Dionysus and 'make a joyful noise to the rock of (their) salvation.' So, brandishing the sacred thyrsus, they run through the consecrated groves beatings cymbals, 'leaping and dancing,' until they have worked themselves up to such a state of religio-sexual hysteria and savagery that when a sacred bull, which animal is thought to incarnate the deity, is driven into their presence, they pounce upon it, tear into it with tooth and nail, eat of its living flesh and drink of its flowing blood. That is to say, they tear their way into the very being of their god, and eat and drink of his divine essence. Before secular law, which is almost solely responsible for such 'purifications' of religion as are ever brought about, made the practice a grievous civil offense, it was not uncommon for a person to serve in the role now imposed upon the sacred bull. There were those who even sought the 'honor.' Worse still, it was not an unheard of occurrence for a parent to throw one of his or her own children into the devotional melee, then dive in after a goodly mouthful or so.

"Even more illustrative of our point than these rites are

some connected with the worship of Attis and Cybele. Each year, their adherents hold a springtime festival. It begins with a sorrowful lamentation over the fate of Attis, the beautiful youth who, for the sake of a lovely nymph, broke the vow of chastity imposed upon him by the goddess Cybele. This act so angered the jealous deity that, in chastising him, she unintentionally caused him to flee into the mountains and castrate himself at the foot of a pine tree. Lamentation continues for three days while the devotees pretend to comb the mountains for the lost Attis. Then he is found and great rejoicing begins. As the excitement grows more and more intense, sexual energy becomes more and more palpable. Emerging from a heavy dolefulness, the holy music grows impassioned until it becomes a veritable bout of audible coition. It seems to writhe in painful pleasure, pant, grasp, and groan as if upon the point of emission. The priests, all of whom are emasculated after the manner of Attis, become so overwrought in their terpsichorean efforts to match action to rhythms that they pelt each other with clubs, and slash themselves and each other with bared knives. Onlookers who are drawn to these rites solely out of curiosity have been known to get so inebriated by this music, these dances, the example of the priests, and the sight of the flowing blood, they strip off their clothes, seize swords placed about for the purpose and geld themselves to the glory of the god, an often lamented but irrevocable sacrifice."

"Pardon, Demias," entreated a legionnaire. "I meant to tell you this before, but I forgot. In Capernaum the other day, I happened upon two of the disciples of your friend the Nazarene. They were debating a saying of the Messiah's one of them had committed to memory. I made him repeat it until I too had memorized it, in order to hand it on to you. 'All men cannot receive this saying, only they to whom it is given. There are some eunuchs, who were born such from their mother's womb; and there are some eunuchs who were made eunuchs by men; and there are eunuchs who have made themselves eunuchs for the kingdom of Heaven's sake. He that is able to receive it, let him receive it.' "

Gestes nodded: "Despite his claim of being the son of Yahweh, who as you will recall wouldn't so much as allow a castrate in his temples, I am not greatly surprised; not after another saying of his which someone was kind enough to bring to me. He said of himself: 'I am the door.' "

"Which means what?"

"In the holy scrolls of the Phoenicians, we repeatedly run across mention of the Asherah. This is either a stump or a tree with its branches stripped off, in which there is an elongated opening. At the upper extremity of this opening is an emblematic representation of the clitoris divided into seven parts. Around it are thirteen tufts of hair, one for each period of fertility a woman goes through in a year's time. This fissure, replete with carvings and adornment, is called the 'Asherah' or the 'Door of life.'"

"Well, all I can say is this," concluded the soldier: "If the Nazarene hasn't already had his 'branch' stripped off, someone sure ought to do 'it' for him."

"I don't know," said Gestes. "Some religionists do as complete a job with their faith as could ever be done with a knife, but do let me finish. I'm in a bit of a hurry.

"The sexual instinct, when otherwise frustrated, often seeks and finds a substitute in religion. There is an interrelationship between the spiritual and purely physical procreative impulses. The story of religion in no small measure is one with the history of the sex urge and its influence upon creations of the imagination. Much the greater part of religious architecture, symbols, rites, and doctrines are of phallic origin.

"Temple pillars, spires, and towers are all symbols of the

phallus. From the particular style of pillar, spire, or tower found in a specific temple, much can be deduced concerning the worship to which it is dedicated. To cite the example of the two pillars: Jachin means 'to be hot with desire'; and Boaz means 'in him there is strength.' The towers, according to First Kings, rose before Solomon's temple, surmounted by chapters which extended up into pommels shaped like water lilies. From that double-sexed image, the Lingam penetrating the Yoni, we are once more reminded of the androgynous nature of Israel's god.

"The tonsured head of a priest symbolizes the head of the virile member. Where could one find a more perfect Lingam-Yoni than is formed by a prelate's bald pate run through the almond shaped collar of a surplice or robe?

"Despite the Law's forbidding 'graven images,' there has never been a time when Jewish temples and synagogues have been wholly devoid of them. Almost without exception, these 'graven images' have been of a phallic or yonic origin and significance. You have no doubt noticed above every house of Yahweh there appears a six-pointed star formed by the junction of two triangles: 'the Sacred Male Triangle' with apex upward like the one formed by the pubic hair of a man, and the other with the apex downward like the one formed by the hair on the Mons Veneris; the two conjoined forming the famous Seal of Solomon and symbolizing the act of coition.

"In the holy of holies of Solomon's temple was a large phallus, 'the Rock of Israel.' According to First Kings, on the ten bases of this same temple, round about graven images of lions, palm-trees and cherubim were figures of the lingam and yoni *K'maar Ish U'lyoths,* or 'like the male and female in embrace.' In other lands and cults arks are sacred—the most sacred object connected with the worship of Osiris is the ark, container of the divine symbol of life. Like those arks, the much storied ark of the covenant, the oblong chest of Shittim wood overlaid with gold in which 'the Rock of Israel' reposed as he was borne out of Egypt and toward Canaan, symbolizes the yoni.

"You have heard, 'Yahweh is a jealous God.' Listen to this: When David and his followers came to Nachon's threshing floor, Uzzah put forth his hand to steady the ark of God, and, fearing it was going to overturn, took hold of it, for the oxen that pulled the cart on which it sat were slipping. 'The anger of Yahweh flamed against Uzzah; and God smote him... and he died on the spot.' Moreover, 'he smote the men of Bethshemesh, because they had looked into the ark (taken liberties with the wife?) of Yahweh, even he smote of the people fifty thousand and threescore and ten men.'

"The cross, one of the oldest and most widely venerated of all religious images, originally had 'cross-arms' at the base; that is, they are now 'cross-arms,' but at first were two round stones that originally appeared at the base. The representation was later inverted that it might better be seen.

"In *The Book of the Prophet Ezekiel*, we read how the daughters of Israel once took their jewels, their gold and silver, and made dildos, tau crosses, of them, 'and did commit whoredom with them.' The daughters were by no means innovators of this practice. The cross has been used as a godemiche since Priapus alone knows when. While in India, I was fortunate enough to witness the ceremonial defloration of a young woman with an ivory cross.

"Circumcision had its beginning, probably among the Egyptians, as a phallic sacrifice, I need not comment upon the part this operation plays in Judaism to this day.

"In their rites of regeneration, Persians make an image of a sacred cow, their female principle, enclose the new convert in it, then drag him or her out through the vulva to 'a new life in

God.' Other cults use water as the penetrable feminine symbol, the head or body of the convert is the masculine, and the significance of the rite, regeneration or baptism 'in God,' becomes apparent.

"Cocks, bulls, goats, pigs and rams have, since earliest time, taken their places among the gods because of their exceptional salaciousness and the envy they inspire in the religiously inclined.

"Before Ano, Bel, and Ea, probably the world's first holy trinity and the antitype of all others was Asher, Anu, and Hoa, the penis with its right and left testicle, man's triple organ of procreation, three gods to one creative purpose."

"Now, there's a god I can believe in," declared one of the soldiers. "And, to think this Jeshu, a religious leader, would advocate... Well, perhaps he ought to be deprived of at least two members of his holy trinity."

Gestes raised his hand. He was not yet finished. "A history of religion which does not devote at least one chapter to the sense of smell cannot be complete. The odors used in temples as incense are the same as those used in brothels as aphrodisiacs.

"When saviors such as Mithra and Krishna were born, they were visited by 'wise men' bearing gifts of frankincense and myrrh, the same odors which Greek and Egyptian courtesans put on their pudenda to excite sexual desire.

"The regulation of sex taboos is the most prized and most jealously guarded function of all priesthoods the world over. Religion does not, as is commonly supposed or claimed, incite sexual modesty and restraint, or a rational sex ethic, but quite the contrary. Wherever you find an abnormal religious zeal, you are very apt to find with it inordinate sensuality, and vice versa. Erotomania and religious mania are sometimes the same ailment. Religion, besides being itself largely a type of sexual aberration, has played a role in the spreading of other such aberrations.

"I need not comment on ideas like 'the sanctity of marriage,' or 'holy wedlock,' as you are all aware of the extreme value placed upon them by the priestcraft. When prostitution ceases to be a source of temple revenue, it immediately becomes the foremost of abominations unto the Lord. And why? Why should this particular occupation be singled out for special priestly condemnation when it has no greater potentiality for evil and quite as great potentiality for good as do numerous others? Simply because, of all the commercial enterprise, it offers religion its keenest competition.

"In this connection, I might call your attention to a subtlety in the method of our friend Jeshu. He is callous toward 'respectable' women, as witness the wedding feast in Cana, when he turned on his own mother who had made the simple observation that there was no wine in the house with the sneering retort: 'Woman, what have I to do with you?' But he is not hostile toward harlots. Rather, he is ever ready to forgive them their past transgression if by so doing he can get them to 'go and sin no more.' That is, if he can get them to discontinue offering him competition.

"The one who associates religion with higher sexual morality ignores the historical fact there is not a single loathsome venereal practice which has not at one time or another been sponsored by a religious cult. Things descried and forbidden, even things punishable by death in secular walks of life, are frequently praised as evidence of great faith when committed in the temples or services of the gods. Absolutism, one of the most highly esteemed of religious creations, by its very nature, spawns all manner of extremes, extremes which in sexual manifestations range all the way from rigid asceticism to complete abandon.

"In all my travels, east and west, I have never found a cult that has not been either grotesquely positive or negative in sexual matters. Whether positive or negative phallicism begets the greater wrongs, indelicacies, and tragedies would be very hard for me to say. What does seem irrefragable to me is the abolition of both would be an unmixed blessing. Until the time that man started to worship the genitals, first those of an animal, probably the bull or goat, and then his own perhaps as symbolic of the generative power of the sun, the act of conjugation was looked upon as a bodily function, the physical response to a physical urge, synonymous with eating, drinking, and breathing and, as such, entailing nothing more unclean or revolting than certain processes of digestion. But, whatsoever religion touches, it debases; it is a sort of accursed alchemy whereby the most precious of metals are converted into the most despicable. And, the one thing which has suffered most from this divine alchemy is the sex life of human beings. Once coition was sanctioned by supernaturalism or absolutism, which must have everything in a supernatural or absolute quantity, the wildest, most gluttonous promiscuity was looked upon both as proof of the most fervent devotion and as a sign of god's blessings. Just as the sex element in religion gives it a universal appeal, so the religious element in sex gives it an aspect of indecency. Among self respecting people there is nothing vulgar or lewd in the sex act but religion probably put it there.

"Seek out the largest temple in any land, and chances are ten to one you will find the land's largest bawdyhouse. In the chief temple of olden Babylon, *Bit-Shaggathu*, literally the Temple of Copulation, high priests rolled in the dust with high priestesses during the new year's rites to promote fertility. Sometime, when you haven't anything better to do, read the books of the Maccabees. The Temple of Yahweh in Jerusalem is the largest lupanar in Palestine. It has no fewer than one hundred little cubicles about eight by five feet, three tiers in height, surrounding the inner scared chamber. Each cubicle is occupied by a *kadeshah* or consecrated courtesan.

"Cults that are negative in regard to phallicism, by discouraging or prohibiting a normal sex life, encourage an abnormal one.

"Greek legend tells us that Bacchus, the god of drunkenness and debauchery, besides introducing among men the use of wine, traveled widely and everywhere taught people to indulge in wild orgiastic excesses, thereby popularizing all those supersensual practices which we call perversions. I realize this is a myth, but like so many myths there is a very substantial truth behind it. The vast majority of perversions are the result of teachings; there are, of course, some congenital cases and gods or priests-of-gods have ever excelled at these teachings.

"Bestiality is probably indulged in the world over by young lads and lonely or timid men, and for the most part is no considerable evil, but religion renders this malpractice a blessed performance.

"At Mendes, in Egypt, living goats are kept as representatives of the generative powers. Men and women resort to the temples consecrated to these shaggy deities and devotedly copulate with specimens of the different sexes trained to enjoy such sacred rites. Herodotus saw these ceremonies publicly performed during his travels in Egypt. He deemed them prodigies, but it is altogether possible that he was the only one in the audience who was shocked; in fact, the only one who did not view the sacrament with all the awe and reverence common to the religious when contemplating their particular rituals. Moreover, if such things are ever meritorious, this ceremony might be said to have been since it no doubt afforded an edifying spectacle to a devout people.

"Lest I mention the evils he sponsored but not those he condemned, I might say Yahweh forbids his children to bring unto him 'the price of a dog,' thereby evincing his dislike for devotional sodomy.

"Lest I mention the evils he condemns but not those he sponsors, I might point out besides *kadeshoth*, consecrated women, there were in the Temple of Yahweh in Jerusalem a number of *kadeshim*, consecrated male prostitutes.

"Herodotus says in his writings: 'People of all nations, except the Egyptians and the Hellenes, are accustomed to copulate in holy places, and proceed after intercourse unwashed into the temples; and they are of the opinion men resemble animals, and every one sees beasts and birds copulating in the temples of the gods and in the consecrated groves. Now, if this were displeasing to the gods, the animals would not do it. Men, therefore, do this and give this reason for it.'

"I do not know why Herodotus excepted Egypt in his generalization, and as for the Hellenes, we need but look at Corinth. There was a time when the temple of Venus Pandemos in this sanctimonious city sheltered over a thousand hierodules who prostituted themselves either in the temple itself or on the precincts thereof. Moreover, these priestesses, who horizontally added so much to the enjoyment of religion, conducted the world's most famous College of Coition. From the far corners of the earth, ambitious and devout women flocked there to learn the innumerable ways these dexterous votaries had contrived for offering sacrifices to their tutelar goddess."

"That reminds me, Demias," said another soldier, "of a story I once heard. Although it is not the account of an actual happening; nevertheless, I believe you will agree it has merits. A Brahmin priest and an Egyptian priest, both connoisseurs of coition, fell to arguing about who was the more versatile in approaching the gate of Venus. To settle the debate, it was agreed that each priest would enumerate in writing all the many positions known and used among his people. Then the two lists would be compared and the matter settled. After this was done, it was found that, whereas the Egyptian had mustered two hundred and forty-three positions, the Brahmin had only two hundred and forty-two. Since a people's honor was at stake the two lists were carefully balanced one against the other, and it was discovered that the Brahmin had forgotten to list the normal position."

"Very good," smiled Gestes. "Your mention of the Brahman reminds me of something. Those of you who have known me for some time may have chanced to hear me utter some dubious remarks about virgin births, especially the virgin births of gods. Don't get me wrong. Although born a skeptic, I am always willing to accept anything for which I can find sufficient evidence. While in India, I heard of an authentic case of virgin birth. There were two beautiful young women living together, neither of whom had ever been with a man, neither of whom had the least desire to ever be with a man. One of these maidens, like the poetess Sappho, had an elongated clitoris and with it satisfied both herself and her companion. The course of true love seldom runs smooth, and not infrequently the cause of its tempestuousness is financial. So it was with these two. The time came when the more aggressive of them had to go out after the wherewithal to buy food and clothing. Being quite attractive, she soon found it. After spending a most nauseating night with a village reveler, she returned home the next morning to spend a much more delightful hour with her girlfriend. To make a long story short, she impregnated her virgin companion with the semen still on her clitoris."

"Go on," objected the soldier incredulously.

"I'm serious," assured Gestes. "This is neither scriptural truth nor holy writ; it actually happened."

The soldier shrugged. "So you say."

"Anyway," continued Gestes, "although I have touched upon it already, there is one element of phallicism, religio-sexual sacrifices, to which I would like to return your attentions.

"These are of three main varieties: those wherein the sex act itself constitutes the sacrifice; those wherein the fruits of the act are offered up for sacrifice; and those wherein the organs with which the act is performed are sacrificed. Of these varieties, it would be very hard to say which has the most hellish history.

"The second, in which the gods of generation are given the first fruits of the 'immortalizing act,' is one of the bloodiest and most exasperating practices in the annals of man. That any human could ever revere a deity who required the sacrificial death of the first-born child as propitiation; that a human pair could beget an offspring in the knowledge that it must serve such a purpose; that anyone could be selfish enough to purchase his or her salvation at the price of another's agonizing death; these would make any self-respecting individual want to deny kinship with the race. Yet the Phoenicians once commonly offered their firstborn to conciliate their gods. So did the Carthaginians. So have others. Even now every firstborn Jewish child, if a son, goes to the priesthood of the temple, and the father has to redeem it from the *kohen*. All the first fruits of a Hebrew's harvest goes to the temple priests. To think of the fruitless waste of lives upon sacrificial altars, the needless agony endured, and the bestializing influence exerted upon those making such sacrifices would be sufficient to discredit anything with anybody, even religion with the religious.

"The story of cultistic mutilations of the sex organs, male and female, is only slightly less degrading. And about the most we can say of 'sacred prostitution,' probably the most ancient and most prevalent of all religio-sexual phenomena, is that it is less bloody. This practice was borne of the desire to sacrifice to the gods one's most prized possession; and the hymen, frail guardian to the 'Door of Life,' since it can be given but once, is especially sacred to the god of generation and must be sacrificed on his altar.

"Herodotus tells us that in his day every daughter of Phoenicia was obliged to go, once in her life, to a temple of Mylitta, and there take a seat under a suspended sprig of mistletoe and offer herself in sexual union with a stranger. Once there, she could not leave until the sacrifice was made. Nor could she refuse herself to any man who, finding her under the sacred mistletoe, would contribute a silver coin to the temple revenue. Some women derived such a devotional satisfaction out of this sacrifice, they were wont to repeat it over and over again. And the priests, finding it one of the most profitable of all yields of superstition and ignorance, were not at all backward in capitalizing upon these pious longings. Quite the contrary. What more praiseworthy means of raising the necessary funds for their maintenance could be employed than cashing in on sanctified indulgences in the 'immortalizing act'? And, since it is the most enrapturing and devotional of all human actions, 'the consummation of God's will,' where more appropriately than in God's temple could it be performed?

"As I have said, the temple of Jerusalem had one hundred cells for the use of 'consecrated' men and women. In all but name these people were sex slaves. They were held by force so long as they appealed to any of the varied desires of man, after which they were eliminated, most often by strangulation, although they were sometimes married off to devout bucolics who considered it an honor to wed one of the god's women. Yahweh himself commanded Hosea to: 'Go take unto yourself a wife of the whoredoms.'

"It is in India, possibly its birthplace, that delubral hetaerism has had its most luxurious growth. The priests in certain parts of that hypocritical country have brought their followers to believe it impossible for a virgin to enter Paradise. What is more, they have convinced their followers only when made by a priest is a hymenal sacrifice acceptable unto the god. Of course, the priest must be well paid to make it. Daughters of the poor remain virginal longer than do those of the more prosperous simply because it takes them longer to accumulate the price of defloration. It is no uncommon sight to see a groom bring his virgin bride, together with the stipulated price, to one of these holy men and stand reverently by while she is deflowered.

"In other parts of India, young women are taken to the pagodas and told a god will appear unto them, woo them, and reveal unto them certain sacred truths. Then, under cover of darkness, Hindu priests impersonate the expected deities. The deluded girls, after their defloration, go out and disseminate as revealed truth all those lies which a people must believe if they are to continue their pliancy to sacredotage.

"In Malabar, even the queen has to submit to the right of relibation exercised by the high priest, who has a right to the first three nights and is paid fifty pieces of gold besides for his trouble. What fools have the gods made of mortals?!"

"By Jupiter!" exclaimed another old veteran. "I'm just now beginning to find a solution for an enigma that has bothered me. For years I've wondered just how it was the priesthood robbed, or rather relieved the army of a certain type of reprobate."

"It's simple," said Gestes. "And, now let me read you a last item from the Song of Solomon: 'How beautiful are your feet with shoes, O prince's daughter! The joints of your thighs are like jewels, the work of the hands of a cunning workman. Your navel is like a round goblet, which wants not liquor; your belly is like a heap of wheat set about with lilies. Your two breasts are like two young roes that are twins. Your neck is as a tower of ivory; your eyes like the fishpools in Heshbon, by the gate of Bathrabbim... Your head upon you is like Carmel; and the hair of your head like purple... How fair and how pleasant are you, O love, for delights.' "

Looking up from his reading and noting the rapt expression on the face of a young soldier, Gestes said: "You evil-minded devil, I'll wager you are thinking this is a song of a man to a woman."

"Well," said the soldier with anticipated disappointment, "I hope you are not going to spoil it for me by saying it is the song of one woman to another."

"Certainly not," said Gestes. "Remember this is holy writ I'm reading, not vile pagan poetry. The Song of Solomon is an allegory wherein the picture of carnal love is a disguise for a divine theme. The wine therein mentioned is a symbol of the Law. The thighs are the Torah, and the belly the Book of Leviticus. The passionate lover is not a rustic swain but Yahweh, and the beloved, 'how fair and pleasant,' is Israel, chosen by the 'Rock' as his bride."

"Which is worse still," sighed the soldier. "As you once said: 'There is no accounting for tastes either among men themselves, or among the gods they create.' With certain exceptions, most of which are female, I'll be damned if I can feature even Yahweh finding in the Jews anything about which to wax so passionately eloquent as all that. To me they are one of the most unpleasant races I have ever contacted."

"You must admit," Gestes said, "that Jew is the world's most studious kleptomaniac. He has a positive genius for stealing without knowing he does it. Seeing or hearing something he likes, he turns his back and originates it. If it happens to be of a religious nature, he gets on a spiritual drunk and has God reveal it to him. You notice this in the sudden outcropping of prophetic and theological talent among the Jews just after their Babylonian captivity. Their priests and prophets, at that time, originated or had revealed to them practically everything Zoroaster taught.

In Second Samuel, which was written before this exile, Yahweh commanded David to number the people, then accused David of having done it of his own accord, and killed seventy thousand of those numbered, which is another example of Divine Injustice. In First Chronicles, written after the exile, it is Satan who suggests this census-taking instead of either God or David. Between the writing of the two books, the Hebrews borrowed from Zoroaster his creation, the Devil. They even retained the Babylonian name. Satan is the Hebrew equivalent for the Persian name which Zoroaster, when he concocted him, gave this dread personage: 'The Adversary.' At the same time, they borrowed the name and idea of Paradise. Before that, dead Jews, good and bad alike, went to Sheol, a vague region beyond the grave wherein souls, forgotten by God, lingered for an indefinite period in a state of unrelieved ennui. The Children of Israel also borrowed from the teachings of Zoroaster, through divine inspiration, the ideas of the final triumph of Good over Evil, of a single all-powerful god, of the existence of evil spirits and guardian angels. By accepting these chimerical scapegoats, they were able to shift problems from their own shoulders to a universe alive with demonic spirits, a process of the eventual coming of the Messianic Son of Man and of a Final Judgment and the resurrection and rewarding or punishing of the dead.

"I'm not saying such is the case, but I wouldn't be a bit surprised if the Song of Solomon has a similar history and these works—there are a score or more poems united to make this supposedly unified whole—were originally the songs of some Babylonian Sappho or Sotades. This suspicion is strengthened by the fact that there is at least one Persian word which Jewish plagiarists or translators have failed to cull out. There is no spiritual element in them from beginning to end; the name of Yahweh is nowhere introduced, and there is no reference to any event in the history of Israel. No especially Jewish customs are mentioned; and many of the geographical localities mentioned are foreign to Palestine. If without so much as one mention of either a religious belief or rite, they still suggest any worship, it is not of bloody Yahweh, but of some such deity as Thammuz or Adonis."

"Be that as it may," said another soldier, "it gives me a marvelous idea. I know a certain seduction story—it is the best one I have ever heard which, restricted as it has been to an audience of soldiers, has never exercised its proper function in the world. With the Hebrew's interpretation of the Song of Solomon in mind, one could take this narrative, let the hero represent incarnate Zealotry; the girl, Heathen; a definite part of his anatomy, the True Faith; a definite part of hers, The Contrite Heart; and he would have a most deliciously moral parable, wherein is illustrated the persistent efforts of Zealotry to inculcate The True Faith into The Contrite Heart of Heathen."

"Oh the ironies of religion," sighed Gestes. "I came over here in the interest of skepticism only to find I have inspired a scripture writer."

"Come to think of it," smiled another of the soldiers, "it is too bad, seeing we Latins have no sacred books, that Ovid was not more religiously inclined. Judging by choice passages in *The Loves*, and *The Art of Love*, he could have written to a god's taste."

"Now that you mention it," I said, "maybe Ovid did mean his works as holy writ. Not that I believe it after what we are hearing, but I have heard *The Art of Love* acclaimed the vilest book ever written, and I happen to remember Ovid makes mention therein that he was inspired by the gods to write. In *Love's Remedy* he tells us in some detail of how one of the gods came to him and whispered a maxim, which he proceeds to quote: 'Let every lover balance the favor and the ills of an amour, and he will be cured of his passion.'"

"Which," laughed a young Roman, "show gods know nothing of lovers."

"Were it not for one verse of Ovid's," said Gestes, "I might suspect Servilius was right. But this one line proves him to be intellectually much too honest for a theologian: 'My certainties are frequently just paradventures.' Since we are speaking of love in general and the love of god in particular, I want to recite for you another of my lyrics, my masterpiece.

"This being my first attempt to translate it from the original Greek, it may sound more like broken-up prose than verse, but first I want to ask how many of you have ever seen a tapir?"

None of us had.

"I've seen but one, myself," said Gestes. "He was in a Carthaginian park, imported there, I believe, from somewhere in the Far East. I can't very well describe him, but it isn't needful. After hearing my poem, just exert your imagination to the utmost, and you will hit somewhere in the neighborhood of this animal's appendage. Unfortunately, I had to give my poem a humorous title. Don't be misled. I might as well admit, skeptic though I am, since my lyric would betray me anyway, that this poem was inspired by a truly religious emotion, was written in all reverence and in a moment of almost superhuman, clear visioned truthfulness.

> **Theology in a Zoo**
> The greatest thing
> I have ever found
> To evince the love of God
> For an earthly creature
> Is the sex organ
> Of the male tapir."

"That's just like you poets," laughingly objected a young soldier. "You always pick your subject from among some far away, uncommon something-or-another. As a matter of fact, I'll bet your tapir hasn't got a thing on a common jackass."

"Don't be bragging on your own kin," said Gestes. "I tell you, God loved this animal! Beside a tapir, a jackass is well, just a jackass."

3

Arising, Gestes replaced his coat about the stone, took it under his arm, and said: "I'm sorry I can't stay longer and read you fellows some more holy-written filthy stories, especially those of King David's son, Absalom, cohabiting with ten of his father's wives on the house top 'in sight of all Israel'; or of old Father Noah's being found asleep and 'humiliated' by his younger son; or of Lot's difficulties in saving two angels from the sodomitical inclination of his townsmen. It so happens, I'm on my way to Tiberias. After so long a time, I have succeeded in convincing my worthy pupil, the Centurion, there is a book which no teacher should be without, and since I cannot afford it myself, he should buy it for me."

Turning to me, he asked: "Would you care to come along?"

Once we were underway, I said, "You know what, Demias? This satiric method of yours no doubt has its merits, but it has its deficiencies as well. I'm afraid it confines you too much to iconoclasm. It succeeds very well in making known the things you do not believe, but what of the things you do believe?"

"I'll admit," smiled Gestes, "they are quite conspicuous for their absence when arranged along with those I either positively disbelieve, or, at least, hold in doubt, and yet, they do exist. Just which of them are you worried about?"

"To begin with, those about these holy scrolls of Israel. I have read several of them myself and I readily admit, despite what you have just been saying against them, that I enjoyed parts of each quite considerably."

"Parts of each, yes," said Gestes. "So have I. What is more, I have enjoyed all of several. As a lascivious song of carnal love, I know of nothing written, not even by Sappho, which I would place above the Song of Solomon. But as holy writ—that is, as an allegory such as the Jews would make of it... Well, every time I so much as think of it, something in me squirms. How often do over-sanctimonious or pietistic minds engender obscene literature. The Book of Ruth is a beautiful narrative if read as such. Shorn of the many priestly additions and corruptions which now so mar it, that part of *Qoheleth* is one of the most invaluable presentations of the pessimistic philosophy ever written. The Book of Job, many of the Psalms, some of Proverbs, and in fact, some of most of all these books are of decided excellence so long as they are not read as the inspired 'word of God.'

"Neither as such nor as a source of either humor or enlightenment, have I any objections whatsoever to pornographic art. In its place, and, I am ready to concede it two or three highly commendable places—it is a priceless stimulus for frigid or jaded passions; it often offers a relatively harmless release for the potentially virulent sexual hunger of the degenerate; and it furnishes us a most enlightening commentary upon the people who produce it—it is not distasteful or detrimental. But I somehow feel, if such there be, should the Creator of poets like Homer, Sophocles, and Lucretius, ever go in for authorship Himself, He would choose another type of literature. Even were He to try his hand at erotica, I still can't feature Him doing such a miserable piece of it as is, for example, the story told in Judges of the Levite whose 'concubine played the whore against Him.'

"No, Servilius, as hard as it may be for you to believe, one of my chief reasons for abusing these books is the hope I have of helping to so secularize them, they will not be spoiled for others as, to a degree, they have been for me by the persistent echoes of such nonsensical assertions as, for instance, these I once heard made by a Magdalen rabbi: 'These books, each and all, were verbally inspired by none other than the Creator Himself. Every word, every syllable, every letter is exactly as it would have been had God written it with his own hand rather than through human intervention. Every scientific statement in them is infallibly correct, all their history and narrations of every kind are without any inaccuracy.'

"Since the books of Leviticus and Deuteronomy say a hare chews a cud, and since 'every scientific statement in them is infallibly correct,' the hare chews a cud, all other existing evidence to the contrary.

"No wonder they tell me Jeshu, making just such an unreserved acceptance of these books essential to salvation, demands his followers 'become as little children.' Who, except he have an infantile intelligence, could ever put faith in a conglomeration of absurd, contradictory counsels and statements of 'fact'?

"I have here," he added, unrolling a piece of parchment, "certain specimens which I copied for Numba's consideration. Don't get me wrong, I do not claim these passages destroy the worth of the books in which they appear. As a matter of fact they are very trivial. But, they are errors nonetheless, and, as such, they loom large in supposedly perfect works. In Genesis, we are told: 'There is nothing unclean of itself; eat every moving thing.' But in Deuteronomy, we are told: 'Swine, hares, and camels are unclean; you shall not eat of their flesh.' Exodus says: 'The iniquities of the father are visited upon the children,' but Ezekiel says: 'The son shall not bear the iniquity of the father.' According to First Kings and Second Chronicles, the mother of Abijah was the daughter of three different fathers, Abishalom, Absalom, and Uriel.

Equally remarkable is the case of that most hardy people the Amalekites. Saul 'utterly destroyed them!' After Saul's death, David re-annihilated them, 'left neither man nor woman alive.' Forty years later, in a battle with Ziklag, they were all killed again, save four hundred young men. Simeon afterwards slew them. Yet we still have Amalekites with us to this day. A 'most hardy people,' I repeat. Nor was their first slayer, Saul, much less hardy. He 'took a sword and fell upon it,' committed suicide, and 'his armor bearer saw Saul was dead.' Yet in a later book he is nonetheless alive, and re-killed by one of these same Amalekites whom he 'utterly destroyed.' In Second Samuel, we find the anomaly, a childless woman with five sons; 'Michal, the daughter of Saul had no child until the day of her death'; nevertheless, the king took 'the five sons of Michal the daughter of Saul.' Then we have the king who was eighteen years old when he was only eight.

'Jehoiachin was eighteen years old when he began to reign.'
'Jehoiachin was eight years old when he began to reign.'

"This list might be extended to some thousands of examples, but for our purpose, those few will suffice. They show an unreasoned acceptance of this holy writ causes men to violate their own sense of truth. When a supposedly divine authority dictates, people are afraid to acknowledge their own sense perceptions and are forced into all manner of elusive and arbitrary practices. Granted these two statements seem to us contradictory, maybe we don't understand just what they mean. A religionist's attitude exactly. When he catches someone in a lie whom he doesn't want to catch lying, he shifts the blame onto his own lack of wisdom. Therein lies the cause for the often-repeated exhortation: 'Be humble before your God.' In other words, if you catch Him or one of his priests in an error, don't call Him on it, don't even admit it, but humbly acknowledge: 'I misunderstood.' Things which elsewhere, men would realize and unhesitatingly declare to be preposterous, in these books they must unreservedly accept lest they burn in Hell for their independence of mind. The same is true of the believer in the many other sacred scrolls 'inspired' by their God or gods."

"I know you are no respecter of deities, Demias, and I rather admire you for it. I'm not god's keeper, either, but I wish you were a bit more lenient with human beings, even worshipers. Back there in camp a minute ago, you were quite blunt, to say the least, in your comment on the Magi and Mithra, and I happen to know there were several Mithraites among your listeners. They said nothing—you were too much 'the master of ceremonies'—but I could tell they were decidedly discomfited."

"So could I," said Gestes. "How well I recognized the characteristic squirm. In a way, I'm sorry, but... Well, I have never yet known a religionist to refrain from expounding his views simply because he suspected the presence of a skeptic, and I am willing to extend him none of those liberties he would deny me. I stated nothing as a fact for which I am not prepared to offer what seems to me conclusive proof, and if those facts hurt, I'm not forcing anyone to listen to them, but neither am I going out of my way to keep anyone from hearing them."

"You went over very well with most of the boys back there. They enjoyed the thought as much as you enjoy the practice of playing havoc with Numba's superstitions. It leaves me a bit worried. Are you sure you are not going to spoil a good position by it?"

"Not my idea at all," he answered. "I'm a soul physician, not a soul destroyer. But, one must have a patient, you know. I'm going to try to keep Numba just sick of spirit enough he will never feel safe to dispense with my services. For, you see," he added significantly, "I'm beginning to like my job very much."

"Now what?" I asked.

"There is an ancient doctrine," he grinned, "which holds that all souls, before inhabiting human bodies, pre-exist in Divine Essence. Each soul, in this pre-natal stage, consists of a male and a female potency united into one androgynous spiritual entity. It divides when it enters human beings; one half going to a man and the other to a woman. Marital happiness is dependent upon the seeking out and bringing together again of the two halves. I try never to care for things by halves.

"Numba was out the other night, and, in his absence, I learned through a diagnosis—'Ovid was my Master'—the other half of his soul, although by far the healthier, the more beautiful, and the more commendable of the two, was also in want of a physician.

"It is this way: Judaism, for all it no longer admits itself to be, is still a decidedly phallic cult. Regardless of their avowed sexual or theological creed, no people is emancipated from the phallic-worshiper's over-evaluating of sex matters who still must speak with furtive baited breaths about sexual phenomena; who is scandalized by an unconsecrated sexual union, even though performed in private and to no evil consequences; who insist sex, of itself, is either holy or unholy, either the special reserve of God and his ministers or the chiefest snare of the Devil; who can find anything immoral in any sexual relationship which, without in any way injuring others, results in the increased happiness of those performing it. Like the adherents of many other phallic cults, people hereabouts are divided into two factions. The one, hoping to attract the notice of God and thereby win his good will, give themselves up to varying degrees of Fescennine ribaldry, exhibitionism, drunkenness, and a variety of sexual excesses. The other, hoping to avert the envy of their 'jealous God' by abstaining from all gratifications which might make him covetous, humiliate themselves, neglect their persons, and more or less completely renounce—as they mistakenly believe—all sexual delights. In reality, they but forego natural pleasures in favor of one or more of the many religio-perversions such as rigid continence, clitoridectomy, castration, flagellantism, or censorship.

"Numba, since his conversion, has sided very largely with this latter group. He gains what little satisfaction his anemic desires necessitate by masturbating himself in his religion, and, idealist that he is, the emotional eunuch expects his wife to do likewise. Fortunately for me, because she is very enjoyable, she has both too much sense and too much passion to derive any satisfaction from spiritual orgasms."

"This," I said, probably with a touch of that moral indignation we so readily feel and so poorly conceal when a man proves unfaithful to a woman we greatly admire with another we greatly desire, "I suppose is an illustrative example of that 'rational morality' I have heard you speak so much about?"

"Well, not the best possible example, to be sure," smiled Gestes. "According to one of my major principles, 'any act or relationship which contributes to the enjoyment of one or more person without causing distress to any must be reckoned as moral.' And how does this little affair measure up? Five people are involved: you, Numba, his wife, Lais, and I. You are a bit envious, I dare say, but that's no serious matter. Numba's wife and I are entering no complaint. Lais neither does nor ever will know anything about it, and can suffer nothing from it. As for Numba, if I am laying up future trouble for him, as it is likely I am, since I have probably weakened his wife's resistance for successors, some of whom may not be so discreet as should be, although it is against my principles, I still must admit, I don't regret it in the least. In fact, I am rather decidedly pleased with the prospect. I'm that intolerant of religious fanaticism."

"It is more than paradoxical," I said, "that the total absence of religious convictions should so endear one to the gods as it has you."

CHAPTER V

The Book of Demias

1

All was well again with our little group in Tiberias. Gestes was off duty one day and three nights a week, which time he spent with us. As for Lais, that princess of all women, she stayed in their cottage and, with such deftness and quietness that her closest friends scarcely noticed the difference, made whatever readjustments the curtailment of her allowance necessitated.

I am sorry my story demands so little of this woman, for Lais was one of the fairest of her sex I have ever known. As much as can justly be charged against sacred prostitution, it is not without some redeeming qualities, and Lais exemplified all those redeeming qualities. Entering the temple at Jerusalem as a mere infant, she lived there until she was no longer a child, when Gestes stole her away. Most of her life had been devoted to the many arts of pleasing men. Her accomplishments, even after making all due allowances for innate genius, attested to the knowledge and skills of her teachers, hereditary brothel-keeping priests who, from father to son, have for centuries accumulated and handed down secrets of their trade. Her singing was virtually perfect, both in voice and presentation, and Lais knew numberless songs of all varieties. She played the lyre, recited poetry in eight languages, and was a dexterous pantomimist, a clever sketcher, and danced as well with extreme dignity as she did with extreme abandon.

True, I have seen more beautiful women in my time. Herodias, wife of Herod Antipas, was more beautiful than Lais. So was ill-fated Salome, Herodias' daughter, Herod Antipas' grandniece. Nor did I find her especially seductive, although I believe this a failing on my part and due wholly to my friendship for Gestes.

It is as a friend, a hostess, a wit, in short, as a general patron of all things pleasant that I cherish the memory of her. Caius, my friend, you should have known this woman; she would have heightened your estimation of women.

2

You should have known Gestes also. You would have enjoyed conversing with him. He made some interesting observations and held some unique opinions. Not that you would have agreed with all his views; you wouldn't have. Neither did I. Neither did he, for that matter, not from day to day or even from hour to hour. As he once said: "The 'I' who so hates to discontinue his sleep and crawl out of bed early in the morning champions a radically different set of values than that championed by the 'I' who so hates to discontinue his work or pleasures and crawl in bed late at night."

Knowing history as he did, especially the history of beliefs and disbeliefs, of good and evil, and right and wrong, he saw men have always engaged in sanguinary rebellions under the delusion they were striving for freedom, when all they have ever done, or even tried to do, has been to supplant one idea with another, one form of mental slavery with another. Nations have ever been at each other's throats because of their overweening political, moral, religious, or social ideals; and what any nation destroys, over and above what it establishes in the way of those ideals, is very often the measure of that nation's contribution to the betterment of humanity at large.

He saw that life, although it has almost infinite capabilities, has no particular meaning; nature, although it abounds in means, has no final ends; and the human race, though run ever so far and fast, has no single or ultimate goal. Moreover, he saw in history too much of the common frailties of man to find in his failures any considerable element of tragic dignity.

All of which, contrary to what might at first have been expected, made Gestes an enthusiast; at times, it is true, a rather saddened enthusiast but still an enthusiast. His was the rare case of a determined hopefulness born of disillusionment. Being somewhat pugnacious, a bit foolhardy, and decidedly adventurous of spirit, he accepted the challenge proffered a thinking man by the lamentable state of human affairs, and he was made optimistic in his outlook for himself by the very fact he was pessimistic in his outlook for others. As he once put it, "For the man who delights in ferreting out, exposing, and seeking ways whereby to abrogate the imbecilities of human beings, this is just about the best of all possible worlds."

Whereas many philosophers and almost all religionists seek the ways and means whereby to "escape from self," nothing made Gestes more content than to feel, day to day, he was drawing closer to, becoming better acquainted with, and increasing his dominion over his self, mind, and body.

Along with Aristippus and the Cyrenaics, he took pleasures to be the only self-sufficiencies within the grasp of man. He also saw, however, that man's physique is much too frail a vessel for the unbridled play of his emotions; overindulged enjoyments exact a proportionate payment of pain. Since this is noticeably less true of mental than of bodily indulgences, he diverted most of his surplus energies into intellectual pursuits. In a man of his stature, this still left a dangerous residue; and it was in acquitting himself of this he exercised a choice I have never met with in any other thinker. Except upon occasions, he drank very sparingly, ate moderately of simple foods, exercised daily and systematically, maintained an even disposition, and associated with joyful and rational companions. Knowing a man could hold up under only a limited physical strain, since he enjoyed the pleasures of Venus above all others, he forswore lesser bodily dissipations to concentrate on these.

Whether I also held these views, I will say it was immeasurably convenient to have a host who did. It resulted in some of the most resplendent days, or rather nights, in my whole life. How I would love to live over some of...

But I must not digress, especially in that direction. I would never finish. Where was I?

3

One time Lais, together with Sarah bath Esau, gave us a feast at the latter's house in Magdala. Since they happened to fall on the same date, this celebration was in honor of the joint birthdays of Gestes and Azzie bar Johnna.

The two women, both culinary artists, surpassed themselves on this occasion. They prepared one of the most novel and savory dishes I have ever eaten. In glass bowls, they built miniature submarine gardens of surprising beauty out of delicacies, fruits and vegetables. They took shellfish of various kinds—some were still alive—and transferred them into hard pastry shells remarkably resembling those from which they were extracted. These they placed among the edible rocks and seaweeds. Just before calling us to the table, they filled the bowls with a sparkling clear white wine.

Small wooden tridents were given us with which to secure the food. It was a clever idea, wonderfully carried out. Shortly after we began eating, one of the guests suddenly sat bolt upright on his couch and, with an exaggerated display of feigned emotion, said: "By the gods, Demias, I almost forgot to warn you! You had better run home this instant and cage up your chickens before you find them all drowned in their drinking water. As I came in, I passed Jeshu of Nazareth headed this way, and I hear he is working miracles again."

Gestes sat up. "If that blessed, destroying Savior ever comes around me or mine working his accursed miracles, I'll…"

"You'll what?" interrupted Lais. "I honestly believe if the truth were but known, you get so much enjoyment out of torturing that poor fool Numba that you are secretly glad those bothersome hogs of yours are drowned and done with. Especially so since you have discovered the old fanatic can be inveigled into buying books you could never afford."

"I'll admit," said Gestes, "I do prefer my new occupation. That morning in Capernaum, when I met him for the first time, I was all for killing Jeshu, and I rather wish even yet I had. However, my present antipathy for him is largely due to literary causes. For some years now I have been troubled by a diabolical inspiration to write scriptures. I have in my possession, thanks to Numba, an old scroll which greatly incenses my local pride with the story it tells of a religious leader of miraculous conception and virgin birth. Saved in infancy from a powerful and jealous foe, he confounded wise men by his youthful sagacity, was tempted by the devil in the wilderness, cast out demons, cured the blind, and performed many other wonders during his ministry. I consider this story much too beautiful a lie to be wasted, as it is, upon an antiquated, far-away heathen. But, so long as they are alive and lack consistency, magnitude, and profundity, as much as I would like to, I cannot take this old scroll and, wherever it occurs, scratch out the name Zoroaster and substitute Jeshu of Nazareth, Apollonius of Tyana, Simon the Samaritan, or another of our contemporary and local saviors, and take it as the framework about which to hang the precepts of a new religion, the one and only true religion the world has ever known: my own."

Azzie, who had come by his disillusionment somewhat bitterly—he was made pessimistic rather than cynical—seized upon this opportunity to say: "I'll kill the very next devil I either happen upon or can instigate. If I am impaled for it, I'm sure your new religion will be a complete solace. Meanwhile, I'm curious to know what possible beliefs you have retained yourself while destroying all we ever professed."

"I'm sorry I have to forbid your well-intended action," lamented Gestes. "Among the very foremost of all my commandments is this one: 'Thou shall not commit martyrdom.'

"But, before going into that, let us look at the whys and wherefores of this future, corrective book of the prophet Demias. As I see it, every scripture writer heretofore has made the initial and fatal mistake of working under the mal-influence of 'Divine Inspiration.' Ever since Plato, that evil genius of human thought who, by the sheer bewitchery of poetic style, made reputable this way of ascertaining truths, we find fancy, inspiration, revelation, and Platonic reason enjoying such advantages over investigation, judgment, and logic as to cause these latter to all but disappear. According to Plato, the senses, able only to feel or perceive and, consequently, limited to the gathering of phenomena or finite truths, have no part in the greater knowledge. This knowledge, as we see in the *Dialogues*, would have us look upon life as a self-deluding commerce with shadows and, for the Highest Good, would have us overlook all lesser goods, would destroy the individual to make a perfect state, would negate facts for the sake of theories or ideas and falsify particulars for the sake of generalities. Solely by divine inspiration, revelation, or reason—reason with Plato was but a method of giving the lie to the testimony of the senses—can we comprehend the supernatural.

"This being the case, what wonder the further men depart from facts the closer they believe themselves to actualities? What wonder everywhere you go you find men who, like our friend the Nazarene, speak with authority about spiritual matters although they know shamefully little about things mundane? What wonder idealistic falsity should be given priority over realistic truth? For a people of whom the poet Hesiod could say: 'The race is of iron, and its righteousness is in its fists'; of whom wise Thucydides could make the generalization: 'The strong take what they can, and the weak suffer what they must'; what wonder these divinely inspired asses, having an absolute command of everything but facts, should offer us such social abirritants as: 'Love your neighbor as your self; Bless those who persecute you; Forgive your debtors; Resist not evil, but recompense evil with good'? What wonder these men should fail or refuse to see the oneness of divine truth and human folly? What wonder they would try to transcend the sordidness of life instead of trying to get to the bottom of things, and..."

"Yes, what wonder?" interrupted Azzie. "And why not? Is not any thinker conditioned by the pose with which he chooses or is forced to confront the world? Men pose as philosophers, lovers of knowledge, and to what lofty purpose? Is it because they desire a correction of their errors, a liberation from their manias? In some few cases, perhaps. There are those of you who accept withering and inhuman facts in a manner that, to me, seems almost brutal. And why? I don't know, but it is my dark surmise, just as there is a form of abnormal sexual passion in which one finds pleasure in abuse and cruelty inflicted by his or her love, there is also a form of abnormal mental passion in which one finds pleasure in cruelty inflicted by his or her favorite thoughts and theories, a kind of intellectual masochism. But in the normal man, knowledge as a disillusioning agency is bitterly despised. For every one who would accept the truth without cost, there are thousands who demand illusions at any price, even at the price of mental balance. The many always have and, I have no doubts, always will found systems upon 'the substance of things hoped for, the evidence of things not seen,' to borrow a phrase or two from the Mysteries, and all that does not countenance these systems ceases to interest them, ceases to exist for them except as objects of either indifference or scorn. I for one am by no means convinced that it is not our refusal to accept things for what they are, more than any other circumstance, to which we owe the willingness of man to continue his existence upon this none-too-blessed earth.

"After all, Demias, is there not a good chance that the discovery of Truth would prove to be the greatest disappointment, the most devastating act in all history? Would it in any way be subservient to human happiness or betterment to have it generally known the lives of the vast majority of our contemporaries are uneventful, unfruitful, insecure, anxious, limited, blighted, miserable, and it will probably be the same with their children until the end of time? However fortunate we may be as individuals, we still must go the routine way of all life, be born in pain, struggle for what will sustain and enable us to grow into a never-quite-self-satisfying personage, must fight against outward foes and inward decadences, and finally succumb to an annihilating death. Can anything helpful come of our knowing that evil often springs from the very core of goodness; or that the most admirable of all human qualities, the love of excellence, kindness, forgiveness, mercy, and the like, are frequently frustrated by their own natures?

"Knowledge is sometimes a source of certitude; it is much more commonly a source of perplexity. It can be the source of considerable enjoyment; it can also be the source of considerable pain. The truth liberates us, yes. But from what? Is it not too often from some of our most prized possessions: our assurances of self-significance—those rosy absurdities which comfort us as nothing else does—and those glad superstitions which preserve both the individual and society? Is it not very probable, very dishearteningly evident, only in delusions can we find any object in our petty existence, with this possible exception: the grasping of certain momentary pleasures? Are not even these momentary pleasures, for the most part, robbed of their ability to give enjoyment once we realize them to be transitory and to no special purpose? What, but hallucinations, can endow life with any meaning and man with any greatness that is not completely obliterated by death? There are probably thousands of people who realize themselves predestined to futility, who realize life to be a cheat. Are they any the happier for their realization? Wouldn't they be much happier without it? Is Truth more desirable, more comforting, more beautiful than fancy? Is it deserving of such praise as you would give it? With what does it reward its followers, except to turn upon and strip them of all values which make human life bearable? Did ever a great thinker die who did not leave the world asking more questions because of his having lived? Is it not possible that one of the first uses to which man put his intelligence was to invent lying? In short, is it not very likely that Truth, in its hour of ultimate triumph, should that fatal hour ever arrive, will gaze upon the collapse of all societies and the self destruction of all thinkers?

"Barring how to forget, along certain lines we know too much already. We know more than we have any desire or need to know. Some things in this old world are best left unknown. In too much wisdom there is unbearable grief. Knowledge can be satanic as well as salvational. Reason itself cries out against its unlimited indulgence. The worth of anything lies, not in what it is itself, but in the relation it bears to other things.

"If man deceives himself, it is because he has found he needs to do so; because he has found realities harsh and antagonistic; because he has found life is not worth the price it demands in ugliness, ennui, suffering, and defeat unless it is bolstered with beautiful deceits—deceits which are nonetheless realities for existing only in the individual or mob mind. You speak of actualities, 'things mundane,' 'the bottom of things.' Is it not possible, or rather obvious, at least insofar as man is concerned, there are other and even greater realities, things imaginary, things which 'transcend the sordidness of life?' The philosophy, if such can claim that designation, which denies the validity of all those many experiences we call mystical leaves me contemptuously cold.

"I tell you, Demias, man has some grievous complaints against Truth. It reveals to us the fact life is a changeling especially adapted to deceiving us at every turn. The whole panorama of existence is, in the main, but a labyrinth of blighted hopes—doomed creatures wishing not to die—and universal carnage—life sustaining itself at the expense of other life.

"There are times when, as sad as it may be, realizing someone must necessarily desert his tower of dreams and face realities in order to bring this old world out of the woeful messes it gets itself into, I entertain an almost infinite admiration for you devils who, regardless of the grime, are always wanting to get to the bottom of things. Then again, seeing some of the abortions you bring to light, I find myself desiring nothing quite so wholeheartedly as to lead every last one of you out and show you Gehenna, Jacob's Well, or the Mediterranean Sea."

"Your sentiments, Azzie, are by no means either original or individual," said Gestes. "Who knows better than I how fatiguing it is to stand forever upon one's own feet, and to shoulder alone, or with only such assistance as one can enlist from his neighbors, those manifold burdens that weigh down the lives of men? This fatigue is one of the pillars common to all temples of religion.

"As I had just started to point out, when you began your Philippic against Truth, much of which, by the way, I sanction in full, and the rest of which with your leave I will presently give my reasons for not endorsing, there are several of these pillars, and we need not rely upon divine inspiration to recognize any of them.

"All theologies, as one can learn by studying the many holy scriptures extant, from the Rig-Vedas on down, are founded upon certain very definite aspirations and fears to which hapless man is an all-too-willing addict.

"Every scripture writer should formulate these, cause and effect, and bear them constantly in mind.

"To begin with there is in human nature, at least in what I conceive to be its baser forms, a determination to believe. Some men are congenital dependents: slaves, parasites, acceptors, believers. They are not ends in themselves; they can discover or create no ends for themselves. Instinctively they subscribe to values which call for self-abnegation. In obedience, they find a positive state of being. In obeying, they flourish. Not to see through their own eyes, not to credit their own senses, not to think their own thoughts but in all things to rely upon others—therein lies their assurance, their strength, their comfort. They are the imminent believers. A glance at history abundantly proves it makes little difference what it is that they believe. Right or wrong, consistent or inconsistent, for better or worse, it is all one; they hold by a thing not because of its worth, but because they want something by which to hold. They are the more dogmatic, absolutist, and final in regard to their beliefs the less able these beliefs are of standing the strain of inquiry.

"One of man's most disastrous failings is his persistence in accepting too emphatically too many things. It discourages curiosity, research, and discovery. It renders an independence of mind superfluous, disadvantageous, or even disastrous. Few people are capable of bearing up under the crushing weight of an absolute conviction. They become automatons, subjects to their enslaving ideals. It has been my observation that the fewer beliefs one has the greater his peace of mind. Certainly, the greater is the peace of mind he permits his neighbors. Life is a comedy for the skeptic; it is a tragedy for the zealot. Fed on the same fare, the one is amused and grows fat; the other is horrified and dies. Where no considerable values are involved, there can be no considerable disaster. Tragedy springs largely from the ruins of destroyed values.

"Closely akin to this determination to believe is humanity's passion for certitude. For all his bold claim to being 'the measure of all things,' man is neither self-reliant nor adventurous enough to like standing alone. He especially trembles to get too far off the beaten pathways of the mind. The unknown is intolerable to little souls. Being too lazy to think and too vain to admit his ignorance, man seeks and finds in religion one answer to all questions: 'God.' Asked the wherefore of such enduring enigmas as Infinity, Space, Time, Cause, Origin, or Destination, he is all too ready with this inevitable stop-gap of ignorance—a stop-gap because it is indicative only of the cringing evasion of an unsolved problem—'God'. A theology not infrequently glorifies stupidity; one always renders stupidities official. By organizing themselves into a cult and preventing, insofar as possible, the spread of any teachings other than their own, men strive to enjoy an honorable irrationality. With ruinous consequences!

"Next—and I wouldn't have you suspect for an instant that in offering it I either disremember or fail to appreciate your late vituperation—there is man's insatiable love of make-believe, his tragic practice of elevating personal desires to the rank of moral necessities. Despising himself for what he is and the world for what it is, he endeavors to escape from both by inventing compensatory fictions and insisting they are the only realities, by inventing all manner of alleviating fancies and insisting they are the only Beauties, Goods, Rights, or Justices. Horrified by the prevailing disproportionate cleavage between what (measured by human standards) is right and wrong, good and evil, perfect and imperfect, he erects teleological blinds to shut out from his infirm mind the harsh glare of actuality, 'things mundane, the bottom of things.'

"An ever present fear of death and an even more exacting fear of life have brought men to stake their destinies on four of the most unfounded and baneful of all human concepts: the immortality of the soul; revealed and final truths; the innate baseness of human nature; and the ultimate triumph of Good over Evil. These have caused men to relegate to God, Fate, Sin, Predestination, Prayer, and other magic formulas, the legitimate functions of intelligence and effort.

"As a result of this self-deification, these man-made Realities, men lose sight of all external or imposed values. They cease to be human, fail to become one with their ideas of God, live like sheep, and die like worms.

"Were it possible for men to change their natures as in a witch's tale, could they, by willing it so, become something else than what they are, then surely we would all be either deities or devils. Since we are the commanders of no such powers, like it or not, we are men, mere men, and ceasing to be men, we become sub- not superhumans.

"Now to get back to my own scriptures. They hold nothing sacred but suspect the very concept of sacredness to be an absurd relic of barbarism. With the best of grace and with no regrets whatsoever, they yield possession of unattainable ideals to other ethical schemes. They do not deny the possible existence of an Absolute, but confine themselves to showing all those now or heretofore worshiped as gods are not divine but pitiable, preposterous, and pernicious. They lay claim to no inspiration higher than that engendered in their author by a desire to better the lot of his fellow men upon this earth and during this life.

"'The Lord is my shepherd...therefore I will do no evil,' say the Hebrew scriptures. 'God is our refuge and strength,' they continue. My scriptures offer no such assurance, underhanded threat, or veiled insult. My god is no shepherd, neither is he a shepherd's dog, an all-seeing, ever-sniffing, meddlesome, dominating cur. He offers no refuge, gives no strength; neither does he spy into my most secret thoughts or condemn me to an eternal Hell for my weaknesses, weaknesses he created in me. Such good works as I perform, I deserve the honor for; and such evil as I do, for that I am accountable.

"As I have said, one of my foremost commandments is: 'Thou shall not commit martyrdom.' The *Book of Demias*, if ever written, will be the *Book of the Living* as contrasted to the old Egyptian *Book of the Dead*. According to Demias, a willing sacrifice of one's life for whatever cause, whether religious, personal, or patriotic, will be the unpardonable sin. This prophet will extend little if any leniency to the man who imagines he has something more noble, more heroic, or more important to do than to live. Since his cult relinquishes all certainty, and for the most part all hope of a hereafter, of future blisses or rewards, it aggrandizes the value of the present, of its positive pleasures and its absence of pains.

"What a tell-tale commentary upon present religions it is that men try to mutilate themselves into a likeness of their deities, to debase themselves into spirituality. Men starve their minds, garrote their passions, and murder their manhood to 'receive it,' that they may be the more acceptable in the sight of Heaven.

"The *Book of Demias*, holding that the well-being of the physiological organism is the final criteria of whatever is ethically valuable and that the most trustworthy basis for an enduring, healthy, and beautiful optimism is a complete outlay of properly functioning vitals, will put an end to all this. Whereas others descry this world, and this life, Demias is only too glad to accept both, and the more of each the better. His concern is not with what we ought to do in imitation of the Most High, but what we ought to do being what we are. He will discourage godliness in favor of manliness. He will inaugurate a change from the worship of the Mutilated Man to that of the Complete Man. Whereas the…"

"Just a minute," interrupted Azzie. "I hate to discourage you, but I'm convinced it is all so useless. Like all tragic philosophers, you offer a sensible system for the guidance of an insensible people. Because supernaturalism has no basis in ascertainable facts; because it is all blather to a mind not blinded by the light of faith; and because it may even be the one greatest obstruction to a certain kind of very desirable human advancement; you make the mistake of denying those compensatory allurements which endear it to the ignorant and credulous; that is, to about ninety-nine out of every hundred of our kind. Man loves the deity who will accept him as a living sacrifice. Possibly the most universal of all religious experiences is the desire to offer one's self, one's energies and one's will upon the altar of the god. It affords the paltry ego a sense of worth, makes it feel itself a cosmic utility instead of the nonentity it too often is. It is this peculiar, flattering parasitism that has ever doomed and will forever doom any and every attempt to liberate men, to inculcate in him self-regard and self-sufficiency. They would much prefer to shine in a reflected glory and escape the appalling responsibilities concomitant with self-assertion. I know this from personal experience."

"You're as pessimistic as an atoning savior," said Gestes. "And I'll admit, I too am at times. But only at times. Therein lies the strength of the Complete Man. He is both a pessimist and an optimist. He is tolerant with both sides of his nature; he takes neither of them too seriously. He is both a materialist and an idealist, sometimes by turns, sometimes both at once. He believes the true reality, insofar as he can know it, to consist of a not-too-dogmatic synthesis of all possible points of view. He glories in future accomplishments, future triumphs, even those he knows will never see fruition. He has his dreams, his moments of self-delusion. It is a childish mind indeed that considers a thing worthless just because it is false. Take for instance some of the beautiful lies we tell and the promises we make to women—yes, and those they make to us. Along with you, he observes nature is completely devoid of any human moral sense, any human mercy. He realizes if there is a god, he makes no perceptible preference between man and rodents. He sees 'doomed creatures wishing not to die, life sustaining itself at the expense of other life,' but he also sees that out of the abattoir, along with cruelty, hatred, gluttony, lust, injury, and death, there comes a very conspicuous beauty. Nor does this latter seem in the least self-conscious, ill at ease, abashed, or debased for its associations with this dread company. On the contrary, it seems to profit as much, or even more, from this internecine and merciless struggle as from any other source. What fails to kill, beautifies. Grant life is a changeling, it betrays us, kills us; it also interests us, amuses and thrills us. Life may be good for no particular purpose; it can still be good, very good.

"The Complete Man does not demand life have any value other than that its pleasures outweigh its pains, its accomplishments outweigh its defeats. Neither does he demand life have any meaning other than that with which he endows it. This does not mean, of course, he would refuse to accept other meanings, could he but find them...

"Since, without a unifying or systematizing element of one kind or another, no organized knowledge is possible, he discovers a unity in things, uses it to the full extent of its worth, but never loses cognizance of the fact he found it, probably only because he put it there to find.

"If not his own god, the Complete Man is at least his own redeemer. He blames no maleficent spirit for the ills that beset him. He blames his own lack of completeness, and he relies upon no supernatural power to right them, but upon natural powers, upon his own facilities, and upon such assistance as he can obtain by cooperating with his fellow men. That he often fails and pays with his goods, happiness, or even his life for his failures is only too evident. But—this is even more in evidence—he does not fail nearly so consistently or so miserably as the man who depends upon God to provide.

"The Complete Man is ready to hear almost any charge against Truth save this one: Truth is less to be desired and more to be feared than Ignorance. He is aware we pay a great price for being humans, for possessing even that little reason we do, but he would rather die a man than live a beast. He would rather advance to a glorious ending than regress to an inglorious beginning. He is conscious of the fact there are no absolutes in human nature, that Beauty, Good, Right, and Justice are different things to different people and different to the same person at different times. He knows, or rationally suspects, the ethical truths of one generation or society may very well be grossly insufficient for the needs of the succeeding generation or another society. He is reconciled to the diversity of his being, and instead of trying to kill certain parts of it and carry them about as corpses, which like all other corpses, putrefy and stink, he cultivates all his own faculties. When they clash, he watches over them to see that no one is the ultimate victor."

"In other words," said Azzie, "this Complete Man is just a restatement of the Golden Mean."

"No," said Gestes. "There is a difference, quite a difference. The Golden Mean, 'nothing in excess,' favors moderation for its own sake. I do not. I value excesses. Nor would I balance them one against the other in order to neutralize the effects of each. Rather, in the clash of opposing faculties I just mentioned, I would determine which should be, not the final but the partial or momentary victor. Did it never occur to you how much men lose by vilifying that almost invaluable blessing we derisively call 'hatred'? It is a veritable fountain of creativeness. A critical, judicious utilization of hatred is almost synonymous with genius. True, an ungoverned excess of hatred is ruinous. So is an ungoverned excess of moderation, love, kindness, or anything else. It is neither the passion nor the excess that is bad but the undisciplined uses to which we put them.

"No, in excesses there is a much desired and seemingly otherwise inaccessible source of energy. This is the one thing I admire about fanatics; their excesses give them an enviable energy. Whenever I want to learn something, I try to become a temporary fanatic on the subject. It drives me on, heightens my interests, enlarges values for me. Later, having gained the desired information, I sober up and right my perspective."

"So that is it," said Azzie. "And all this time I was lamenting the fact you were born among us Jews rather than your own people. I just supposed it was the ill treatment you suffered at our over-pietistical hands while still in your youthful, impressionable years that made you an irreligious fanatic. Well, I'm glad my race is exonerated, although it does leave me grievously disappointed to learn your almost praiseworthy enthusiasm for manhandling the gods is due to nothing more admirable than a vulgar taste, an insatiable lust after truth, a swinish longing to get at the bottom of things."

"It is amazing," said Gestes, "that, sentimentally, men should so often be at such considerable odds with their most rational judgments."

"Yes," said Azzie, "and what is more amazing still is the fact it is probably better thus."

Gestes looked at him and, for the first and only time of which I have any recollection, greeted the avowal of an opinion with a frown. "Incorrigible pessimists like you make it dishearteningly difficult at times for even the most optimistic of us to wish or hope for anything better for you than the gloomy, stagnant existence you would make..."

"'The most optimistic of us,' echoed Azzie banteringly. "Is it possible, Demias, you include yourself in that category?"

"Can you doubt it," asked Gestes, "when I devote my life to

trying to make independent and self-respecting men of the spineless idiots you sometimes pretend to exemplify?"

Azzie shook his head incredulously; "What a skeptic! The man even doubts my imbecility!"

CHAPTER VI

The Miracle

1

Gestes and Azzie were still discussing the merits and demerits of the unwritten *Book of Demias* when we heard a small group of people trooping past the door. Looking out, we recognized the Nazarene at their head.

"Azzie," said Gestes with sudden inspiration, "you get into pitiable shape at times. I often wonder if even a miracle could bring you out a straight man. Now..."

"Oh, no you don't," interrupted Lais. "That charlatan has done us enough harm already. I won't have him spoiling our dinner as well."

"Don't worry about our not eating," said Gestes. "Such things can give one moral indigestion, but they never spoil the appetite. We'll be back."

To Azzie, he said: "If you put on some shabby old clothes and disjoint yourself, you would make an ideal subject for a miraculous cure. I believe you had best be a beggar in order to inspire in him a kindred feeling. Have you any such old dirty clothes?"

"I have some that are dirty enough," smiled Azzie with a sideways glance at Sarah, "and we can readily make the holes."

"Yes," laughed another of the guests, "the holier your clothes the better. And, from what I have heard of his race prejudices, it may be necessary to show the Nazarene your circumcision before he will have anything to do with you."

"But what am I going to say?" asked Azzie as we assisted him in changing his attire.

"Be reverent and supplicating," said Gestes. "Address him by the titles dear to all saviors in all times. Go at it something like this: 'Jeshu, Divine Paraclete, Avatar, Son of the Self-Existent, Giver of Life Eternal, the Logos, the Upright, the Opener, have mercy upon me, a cripple. Have compassion, oh Redeemer, Mediator between God and man, oh only begotten Son of God, see and...'"

"Careful, careful!" interrupted a guest. "Watch out that, being a contortionist, you don't get things twisted up and call him the misbegotten son of something else."

"A wise precaution," said Azzie. "What ever I do, I don't want to incur his curses. I've heard they are so vile they withered the leaves on an overhearing tree."

Finished with dressing, Azzie assumed one of his most distorted poses, and what a pose it was! He hunched his back and threw both shoulder blades out of joint, one upward and one downward, thus completely destroying the natural symmetry of his trunk. He brought his knees in so they knocked together as he walked, and turned his feet crosswise on his ankle with his toes in and heels out causing them to look like knotted clubs. His arms dangled in front of him as if they were something thrown about his neck. He leaned forward like a broken ape, rolled his pupils almost out of sight into the top of his head, and in a cracked voice asked, "Well, how am I doing?

"Great!" admired Gestes. "If this Messiah can bring you

back to human shape, I'll become religious and resume saying my prayers right where my grandfather left off."

2

Gestes and I ran around a number of neighboring houses and approached the Nazarene to his face.

Azzie, on the other hand, with a pained, forward-falling, jerky stumble, followed in his wake, and while still some distance away began to cry out for a cure. He was a natural son of Thespis and played his part to perfection.

Jeshu turned to see who it was that so lavishly praised and so earnestly entreated him. After one glance at the human wreckage behind him, however, he resumed his course.

"Ha!" laughed Gestes. "Our Hebrew Messiah no doubt realizes this man's afflictions are not of a nature to be cured by miracles."

Azzie quickened his lurching pace and caught up with the back of the troupe. So sympathetic did those about him become, they soon joined him in his supplications. The Nazarene eventually turned a second time to confront the supposed unfortunate.

"Now for the Miracle," gloated Gestes. "Watch closely, especially his hands, and see if you can catch on to how he works it."

"Why do you think I can do this thing?" asked Jeshu.

Azzie arose to the occasion admirably: "Because you are the Son of the Father. You can do anything."

"If in truth," said the Messiah, "you believe this thing, your faith will make you whole. Stand up and be as one newborn."

Azzie counterfeited a desperate effort to pull the knots out of himself but held his pose. In a perfect desperation, he looked up to the Redeemer.

Jeshu, seeing he could do nothing for this man, began to curse him for his hypocrisy and lack of faith, saying where there was no belief he could 'perform no great works.' Turning, his nose as contemptuous as a camel's, he started to walk away.

The aggregation of onlooking moral simpletons appeared to be wholly satisfied with this religious farce. They accepted it on faith, I suppose, that if the beggar had received no blessing, it was his own fault.

Gestes, however, hastened up to the Nazarene, and said, "But Master, this man is a special friend of mine. From birth he has been afflicted in this manner. He has never committed any sin! He can't, poor man; he is impaired in that respect also. If his faith is likewise crippled, why, he can no more help that than he can the crookedness of his body. These miracles cost you nothing; perform two of them, one to cure his faith one to cure his body."

Jeshu looked at him disdainfully and started once more to walk away, but Gestes caught him by the shoulder and stopped him. "Wait a minute; you're immortal; you've got lots of time. Spare us a second or so."

For a moment the two looked into each other's eyes with silent defiance.

Suspecting that Gestes, who was given to acting before reckoning its consequences, would soon have us involved in a brawl, I found myself silently lamenting having left my *cingulum militare* where I threw it aside when going to the table.

To my peace of mind, Gestes, as if with a sudden change of intent, stepped back a pace, and said: "Come to think of it, relax a bit. There's something I want to talk to you about. A friend of mine tells me that two Sabbaths ago or less, he caught you and your disciples in his field helping yourself to his grain. Tell me, according to holy writ, to say nothing of civil law, is it not wrong to steal another man's corn on the Sabbath?"

The Nazarene's face, which had become a trifle glum, at this instantly became almost radiant. His followers crowded closer about him. As did Gestes, they knew their master had been questioned upon this same subject by their fellow Israelites on the day of its happening, and recalled with considerable satisfaction how he had squelched his critics. They were childishly anxious to see the thing re-done.

The Nazarene probably remembered his speech almost word for word: "Have you not read what David did when he and they that were with him were hungry; how he entered into the house of God, and did eat the shewbread which was not lawful for him to eat, neither for them which were with him but only for the priests? Know you not it is written in the law how, upon the Sabbath days, the priests in the temple profane the Sabbath and are blameless?"

Jeshu, however, had overlooked the fact that he was addressing no fellow Israelite nor any great admirer of David, Jonathan's giant-killing lover, a 'man after God's own heart,' the Nero of Jewish history, a cruel, deceitful, lascivious, brazen faced adulterer and murderer—in short, the one most infamous character in the too-long list of moral reprobates or 'men of God' with which the holy scroll of Israel acquaints us.

"That's no answer to my question," said Gestes. "Like all gods and priests of gods you give too much worth to authority, especially the authority of the long dead. You accept antiquity as a credential of value. You misconstrue examples for justifications. Great David did the deed you mention. This leader of a band of Ziklag freebooters, by a lie backed up by arms, also usurped the throne of Israel. So did he, during one of his fleeting passions for a woman, have Uriel killed that he might get the good soldier's wife. But, therein lies neither reason nor excuse for you or I to commit the same atrocities.

"One trouble with you gods, sons-of-gods, and priests-of-gods, is that you are badly in need of studying up on your logic. You should read Democritus. Yes, and Aristotle. You can prove anything, given either of two conditions: the first being that your statement is accepted as ultimate truth; the second being that your authority is accepted as irrefragable. Without either one or the other of these concessions—and no thinker would grant you either—like a syllogizer attacked on his major premise, you are completely and hopelessly lost. You utilize only proofs by authority, the very lowest kind of proofs, in fact no proofs at all. With you, positive statements are stronger than facts. You mistake aspirations for arguments, convictions for evidence, and a good intent for a criterion of truth.

"It is due to these errors in logic the proselytes of every faith maintain the inerrancy of their particular rites and doctrines with such furious zeal and bigotry, and condemn those of all others with such finality and violence."

The Nazarene was completely amazed to find an argument which had scored him such an overwhelming triumph on one occasion should, upon exact duplication, be exposed as wholly irrelevant and ridiculous. Being no idiot, he sought to better his answer: "And why shouldn't we, being hungry, eat where we find grain to eat? Behold the beasts of the wood and the fowls of the air: for they sow not, neither do they reap, nor gather unto barns; yet the heavenly Father feeds them. Are not men much better than they?"

"I hate men who think to answer questions by asking others," said Gestes. "As a matter of fact, I don't know whether or not men are better than beasts or fowls. I have my personal opinions on the subject and, generally speaking, I would honor men above beasts, though there are cases when, for instance, I would honor certain dogs and horses above a good percentage of human beings, but I have neither method nor criterion whereby to declare my opinions invulnerable. However, if you will allow me for this once to resort to your type of argumentation, I will say most emphatically: "No, you are wrong, men are not better than beasts, for in *Qoheleth*, it is written: 'That which befalls the sons of men befalls beasts; even one thing befalls them; as the one dies, so dies the other; yes they have all one breath; so that a man has no preeminence above a beast.'

"But, let us put an end to this child's game of silly answers. What I want to know is, will you or will you not cure this man of his inflictions?"

The Nazarene was glum. "All right," said Gestes, "if you won't do this thing, Mithra will."

Turning to the east, he lifted his arms and began this prayer: "Oh Divine Mithra, Savior, Redeemer, Intermediary between God and man, hear your humble servant. Not for mine, but for this poor fellow's sake and for your own, I ask you to do what this Hebrew Messiah either cannot or won't."

Ending this prayer, he turned to Azzie and said: "In the name of Mithra, second member of the holy trinity, I command you: Be of strong faith and of sound body."

With a convulsive movement the contortionist threw his limbs back into their proper places, straightened his back, and screwed his face once more into its natural contour.

For an instant thereafter he stood as if unable to believe in his happy metamorphosis; then, with vociferous rejoicing, he leaped forward, seized the awe-stricken Nazarene by both hands and began to dance about him in circles.

Gestes, who was ready to leave well enough alone, grabbed

Azzie, broke his hold on the Messiah, and, mumbling something about carrying the glad tidings to Azzie's mother, started with him on the run to the house. I followed and would have joined them in their whooping but the expression on the face of one of the Nazarene's disciples stayed my voice.

I have often wondered, could I have read it, exactly how much of future history I could have found written just then in that man's face.

CHAPTER VII

Ironies

1

About a year and a half after Gestes started working for Numba, Jeshu began to make frequent appearances at the synagogue in Magdala.

By this time, fantastic stories of the Nazarene's "great works" were circulating about, and the whole neighborhood was in a frenzy of excitement. As for the centurion, poor devil, he was caught between the horns of a most excruciating dilemma. Although he went to synagogue regularly every Saturday, he understood nothing that was said. He very much wanted Gestes to accompany him and act as an interpreter, but the Mosaic Laws forbade working on the Sabbath, and he suspected interpreting might be looked upon by the Lord as a form of labor. Moreover, he could not ask Gestes to come in from Tiberias as a favor, because the distance was at least twice that which an orthodox Israelite can walk on a holy day.

But there never was a predicament which a fanatical religionist could not conscientiously squirm out of, one way or another. Numba secured one of the very few houses in Magdala into which a man could enter without having to hold his nose, and he offered it to Gestes under such favorable conditions as could not rationally be rejected.

On the first Friday after Gestes' relocation, the centurion approached him to say, "I wouldn't be surprised if the prophet Jeshu of Nazareth were to speak in the synagogue tomorrow. I'm sure you will want to hear him. They tell me he is a most interesting and instructive teacher. Tell me, what do you think of the tales that are going around about him?"

"Which one, for instance?" asked Gestes.

"Oh, any of them," said Numba evasively. "For example, someone tells me Jeshu was once seen to walk on the surface of the Sea of Galilee."

"I hadn't heard that one," said Gestes. "At least I hadn't heard it of the Nazarene. Of course, I have read about Zoroaster walking on water on his way to Mount Iran to receive the law, but I wasn't aware of its having been accomplished since."

"I wasn't aware of its having been done before," mumbled Numba a bit savagely.

"Oh yes," said Gestes innocently. "It has been a rather common occurrence. Gautama, the Buddha, walked across a river; a great number of his disciples witnessed the fact. It's well known that Euphemus could run across water so fast he wouldn't even get his feet wet."

The centurion frowned, but Gestes went on as if unaware of Numba's antipathy. "Now, regarding Jeshu's miraculous, or telepathic, as some would have it, healing of the sick, now that, I'll admit, I don't exactly know what to conclude.

"A cynic once observed: 'Miracles happen only when and where there is a people disposed to believe in them.' The case of Jeshu bears out the assertion. When visiting his native village Nazareth, a while back, finding himself among those who had known him from infancy and who were inclined to regard him more as an idiot than anything else, he was unable to perform his miracles."

"The Nazarenes were not 'a people disposed to believe in them,'" Numba avowed. "A prophet is not without honor..."

"Precisely, so I wouldn't wholly discredit his healing ability. I can't go so far as the Stoic who says: 'There may be matter, but it does not matter that there is,' and yet, I realize there is, unphilosophically speaking, such a thing as the dominion of mind over matter. This same Gautama, the one who walked across a river, made the assertion that a man's peace and salvation came, not from the outside interference of the gods, but solely from the control of his own mind. I believe there can be no doubt but that all a great many people need to be healed of certain ailments is the assurance they are healed. Pythagoras cured great multitudes just by telling them they were well. History even has it he brought men back to life just by..."

"Yes, yes, I know," interrupted the centurion, desiring to hear no more of the famous metaphysician. "You know what, Demias," he continued, completely dismissing from his mind his teacher's data, "you are unusually blessed. You have a marvelous memory, the most marvelous memory I have ever heard tell of. I wouldn't be at all surprised that with a little effort you could recall, if not word for word, at least item for item, a talk you listened to a day or two earlier. Am I right?"

"Well," said Gestes, "I hate to correct my employer in any good but erroneous opinion he might have chanced to form of me, but as a..."

"You're just modest," cut in Numba, determined not to have his point defeated. "With a few notes to remind you, I'm positive you could. You write Greek shorthand, too, don't you? I was about to suggest... But, of course, you couldn't make notes on the Sabbath." He frowned. "I wish it were permissible for you to write down a few quotes. I'd be only too willing to give you an extra day off with pay each week if you could tell me on Sunday what is said each Saturday in the synagogue. This Nazarene has me curious. But, of course, I wouldn't for the world be instrumental in your endangering the well being of your immortal soul."

"I don't know," said Gestes with feigned dubiousness. "I believe, considering the circumstances, I could take a few notes without doing myself any harm and without even letting anyone else know I did it. You see, a number of the Pharisees whose synagogue it is, after all, are contending nowadays that God meant the Laws of Moses to be taken much more freely than certain other Judaistic cults advocate. They claim the Torah is divine, but our interpretation thereof must necessarily be human. I recall hearing one of them say: 'The Sabbath is given unto your hands; you were not given unto her hands.' Furthermore, they contend anything done to the greater glory of the Most High can be done on the holy day. Are they not right?"

"I don't know," said Numba noncommittally. "But," he hastened to add, "you should. You can read the Scriptures."

"Anyway," concluded Gestes, "under the circumstances, I'll take the chance."

2

It was thus arranged for Gestes to take notes on what he heard each Saturday, and he found in this a source of considerable amusement both for himself and for those of us who accompanied him to the synagogue. While writing down the solemn pronounciamentos of Jeshu or some other pious speaker, he whispered translations to us. This was made easier for him by the more or less immutable manner in which the rabbis worded many of their dicta in order that the worshipers, most of whom could neither read nor write, might easily commit them to memory. Whereas the Mosaic laws often start with "You shall not do,..." the Pharisees, seeking to lessen the rigor of their religion, commonly modified the older texts to begin: "Blessed are you who do..."

Gestes invented still another form for his amusement. As usual, there was as much wisdom in his foolishness as there is foolishness in many men's wisdom.

Some of his parodies, I remember: "Accursed are the followers after priests and prelates, for they entrust their salvation to others. Accursed are the meek, for only the kingdom of heaven is theirs. Accursed are the stupid, for they find honor only in the sight of God. Accursed is he who 'speaks as one having authority,' for he is doomed to amuse idlers with his solutions of the unsolvable."

It is one of the ironies of religious history that the Christians, who neither know nor are willing to learn anything of Jewish life, character, culture, customs, or institutions, have made the Pharisees out to be the most bigoted, intolerant, and hypocritical sect of Judaism.

As a matter of easily provable historical fact—there are thousands of existing documents to bear me out—the Pharisees, in contrast with the Sadducees and other literalists, are quite conspicuously revolutionary, liberalizing, and invigorating. They are the only Israelites who have merits sufficient to warrant rivalry, fear and condemnation. As is so often the case in religious antagonism, the Pharisees are singled out by Christians for special abuse, not because of their failings but because of their relative excellencies, those things which make them survive as formidable competitors.

What is more ironic still, Christians have put this venomous ignorance into the mouth of their Christ, who, as a Nazarene, championed the Pharisaical reinterpretations of the old Scriptures; the same Christ who used the very phraseology of the Pharisee in his most cherished sayings; the Christ who taught in their synagogues and criticized them, as they criticized themselves, for their own good.

What unparalleled ironies we find in the story of religions! The gods of the Indians are the devils of the Iranians, and the gods of the Iranians are the devils of the Indians. The Jew begins his prayers by addressing "the One and Only God, Yahweh," whose name must be hidden, and he ends his prayers with "Amen," truly, while the Egyptian invokes "King of the Gods; Amen-Ra." and his "Amen" means "that which is hidden." The Persians, instead of worshiping their deities, do homage to Ahriam and Dew, their devils, on the principle it is better to propitiate an evil spirit than to reverence a good one. Western cults offer as a major proof for the existence of Heaven, a place of eternal life, "Man's universal longing for immortality." With equal hopefulness and dogmatism, those of the far East offer as major proof for the existence of Nirvana, a state of eternal death, "man's universal longing for total extinction."

The devotees of possibly the two most extensive religions on the earth cite as divine truths and holy writ the atheistic denials of their protestingly deified leaders, Confucius and Gautama. Most ironic of all, we now find Roman soldiers worshiping as the Gentile Messianic God of Love that vengeance-hungry Galilean mono-maniac who lived and died in the apocalyptic hope of seeing the world destroyed and Rome with all her legions cast into a hell of fire and brimstone to burn forever in sight of a Persian paradise from which the children of Israel could look down and gloat.

3

I sometimes went with Gestes to the synagogue and on several occasions heard the Nazarene. He was a convincing speaker, having a certain natural eloquence and a winning, one might say an ensnaring, personality. He was absolutely sincere in what he said and entertained no doubts whatever but he spoke from divine inspiration.

His audiences, consisting of mostly ignorant, impoverished, and suffering peasants, along with a few credulous petty officials, were so intoxicated by his hopeful arguments or, rather, statements that, speaking as one having authority, he seldom condescended to offer proofs for his assertions. And so questions were infrequently if ever raised concerning his rationality.

When one stopped to think over his apothegms, however, he readily saw that Jeshu, with his sleight-of-words, had, like the Sophists of Greece, made the worse appear the better reason. He offered as a solace some of the saddest facts of life. For example, he once said with soothing optimism: "Blessed are the meek, for they shall inherit the earth."

It is possibly true the meek will inherit the earth. They have on many occasions in the past. Who, for instance, now occupy the marble halls of which Ninevah was once so proud? Not kings and heroes as of old, but owls and foxes. Mice and lice have inherited the earth that once belonged to lion and tiger.

A short way out of Magdala, near a huddle of limestone hovels strewn along a short dusty white street which smells of fish, there are the ruins of a marble palace, the sole monument of a civilization so long dead and so completely forgotten not even legend tells of its ever having been. Yet, this one marble pillar is all-sufficient to prove the people who placed it there were vastly superior to those now rotting in filth at its base.

I can picture a time when Athens will be but a slab of stone on a mountain's top and Rome but another on a river's bank, and each the inheritance of its present scum or "meek." But in order for a man to find any "blessed" element in such dismal prospects, it seems to me he must be a bitter misanthropist, at least partly mad, or a disparate reactionist.

I would conjecture that, to a degree, the Nazarene, directly or indirectly, was a fit subject for any or all of these three categories. He so loved his own people wherein their oppressors were involved that—since this includes practically every Gentile nation—he was an ardent hater of men.

He allowed desires to necessitate realities to the point of idiocy. For no better reason than it fit into his scheme of things, he taught without any doubts or reservations the world would end within the lifetime of many of his contemporaries. Although plausible enough under his doomsday ethic, it is manifestly ridiculous under any other set of circumstances.

Let us have a brief survey of the circumstances which conditioned Jeshu's character and career.

Palestine, at the time of his birth, was in a most pitiable plight, partly because of the failings of others, partly because of her own failings. In one of the ironies of religion, the Hebrews forced the Idumaeans to accept Judaism. This was their first conversion at the point of a sword—and by so doing they made it possible for the Idumaean Herod to become King of Judea.

What a king he turned out to be! Someone epitomized his reign thus: "Herod stole to the throne like a fox, reigned like a tiger, and died like a dog." In order to get into the royal family of Judea and thereby become somewhat eligible for kingship, he married a Hasmonean princess. Then, in order to rise in the royal family and increase this eligibility, he began a systematic extermination of his in-laws. By clever deceits, the fox gained the aid of Rome, made war upon the

Jews, completed his extermination of the Hasmonean dynasty, and became sole ruler of Judea. Over a hundred thousand men died in the wars which insured his supremacy. Those of this hundred thousand as were Hebrews proved, in the light of subsequent developments, to be the most fortunate of their race for many years to come, for exit the fox, enter the tiger! It is probable not a single day of his reign passed without some cruel act of despotism. Despite a passionate devotion to his wife, because she was Hasmonean, he charged her with adultery and had her executed. Because his five sons by her were also of her blood, he went about having them put to death. "It were better to be that man's pig than his son," exclaimed Octavius Augustus when he learned of these murders. The mystical Israelites came to look upon Herod as an anthropomorphization of evil on earth.

Now, if we may accept Gestes definition: "A messiah is an imaginary savior born of unfulfilled desires," you can readily see why it is that during the days of Herod the King the messianic idea should have become such an obsession with the Jews.

Herod was not the sole source of the Children's troubles, nor did his dying 'like a dog' usher in the millennium. After he died, Rome assumed direct control of Palestine and levied heavy taxes upon it. She had to in order to build the roads and sustain the imperial armies necessary to preserve the peace among this un-peaceable people. The priesthood of Yahweh, the eternal curse of the Jews, was taxing them more heavily still. (As often as the Israelites have formed a state, this priesthood has swallowed it, digested it, extracted all the life giving nutrient out of it, and, finally, excreted it into the slave marts of other nations.) The Hebrews never have and probably never will maintain themselves for any length of time or with any degree of self satisfaction as an independent nation. What time they have not been in slavery, they have engaged in civil war. Once in their long history, during the reigns of David and Solomon, they enjoyed a trivial magnificence due to the fact that Phoenicia plied a successful sea trade, which opened the possibility for them to conduct trade across their land. Nevertheless, this much-overestimated hour of glory gave the Jews an opportunity to exult in their past and yearn for its return. They have ever since made it a point of honor to go backward. They idealize national and economic independence but refuse to realize these are not natural states of man, not gifts of the gods, but things which only a strong and sagacious government can provide. In short, they are a voluptuous, luxury-loving people who desperately desire the goods known and enjoyed by others but are unwilling to allow for the compromises, deprivations, and inconveniences necessary to obtain them. Hence their inordinate craving for, trusting in, and relying upon divine intervention and aid.

For centuries they held to the frenetic hope that Yahweh would walk the earth again as He is supposed to have done in the Garden of Eden, but by the time of Tiberias they had just about given up seeing this (possibly they realized that Rome would not tolerate the bloody brute at large) and transferred their wish-inspired expectations to the coming of the Messiah, Son of God.

Which gets us back to Jeshu and his fictitious divinity.

He had sense enough to see that the Israelites, with their blind and unshakeable faith in the eventual coming of a militaristic savior who would overthrow the rule of Rome and re-establish the Kingdom of David, were headed for racial destruction. Saviors were arising all over Palestine, gathering armies, and leading them to inevitable defeat. In her vain endeavor to govern a race that would neither rule itself nor submit to the rule of others, Rome was showing signs of a galling weariness. Jeshu saw that a passive resistance rooted in the worship of Yahweh was the only thing that might save Jerusalem from going the way of old Carthage and Corinth. Consequently, he preached a "kingdom not of this earth" and a religious conceit which would enable the down-trodden Hebrew, believing his to be the only people chosen for eternal bliss by the one and only God, to feel sorry for, rather than envy the Gentile his earthly wealth and power.

Recognizing that, if those things which they could not hope to have or enjoy were declared ungodly, his people would feel less grievously their deprivations, he launched such a system of negations as has no equal elsewhere in all history. Almost all that is negative, he held to be gloriously positive. He falsified almost all truths, all realities, put faith above reason, acceptance above inquiry, love above intelligence, held abstractions to be the greater actualities, this life but a preparation for another after death, and this world but a painful prerequisite for the one to come. He reversed almost all goods, all values and declared especially blessed of the Most High: poverty ("Blessed be ye poor, for yours is the kingdom of God"); submission ("Blessed are the meek"); un-enjoyment ("Blessed are they that mourn") the absence of family relations ("There is no man that has left house, or parents, or brethren, or wife, or children, for the kingdom of God's sake, who shall not receive manifold more in this present time, and in the world to come, life everlasting"); and ignorance ("I praise you, Father, Lord of Heaven and earth, for concealing this from the wise and learned and revealing it to the simple minded; yes, Father, I praise you that such is your chosen purpose").

Which goes to show the Nazarene was not without a certain logic, a demented genius. But, as a religious leader, he had none of the salubriousness, the originality, or the universality which characterizes men of the East like Confucius, Gautama, or Zoroaster.

By teaching that the soul, an abstraction, is the essential reality in human nature, while the body is a temporary, inconsequential, and rather indecent lodging place of the soul, he encouraged a neglect of health, even of body cleanliness.

He said "Take no heed for your life, what you shall eat, or what you shall drink, nor yet of your body, what you shall put on." He discouraged medicine by his foolish belief in devils, demons and evil spirits.

By making all men equals in the sight of God, he indirectly minimized the worth of self-improvement and of all improvement.

Holding that all worthwhile truth is revealed and never changes ("for ever...is settled in Heaven"), he rated inquiry and almost all learning among the sins of the world for which he was to atone.

One of his fundamental doctrines was salvation by faith alone, a doctrine that imposes no necessity for good works, puts no curb on evil-doing, but allows a believer to commit any crime with impunity—faith will save him from a just punishment—and condemns a non-believer, regardless of how much good he may accomplish, to an eternal Hell.

Being a religious pervert Himself, he jealously tried to win men away from sex-love by making the act of conjugation a matter of filth.

He endeavored to point out to man no way whereby to achieve an enduring peace and happiness, how best for him to conduct relationships with his wife, his employer or employees, his fellow workmen, or his government, or how to prevent wars, famines, and pestilences. He was essentially a god of the much-abused, the infirm. His followers must suffer their distresses that he might heal and comfort them, that he might give them salvation. His cardinal good was not physical or intellectual, but the emotional pleasure to be derived from an almost complete denial of life, reality, and earthly values, the pleasure to be derived from misery.

He said nothing not said (and often better said) before. His ideas about the soul, an immortal ethereal being temporarily imprisoned in the carnal body but ultimately destined for an eternity of bliss or agony, were those of the ancient Hermetic books of Egypt, especially the *Perfect Sermon*. His teachings on baptism are all in *The Font*. His much-ado about the relationship of men to the Heavenly Father, barring his Jewish exclusiveness, are item for item in the Hermetic Scriptures: "His first-born Son to take charge of the sacred flock, as though he were the Great King's viceroy. All men are sons of the same Father. The man of God who, being the Logos of the Eternal, is of necessity himself eternal."

The Gentile who says Jeshu came to save him, according to the Nazarene's own teachings, blasphemes, for as I have already pointed out, he said: "I pray not for the world, but for those given me. I am not sent but unto the lost sheep of the house of Israel. It is not meet to take the children's bread and cast it to the dogs. Therefore, speak I to them in parables: because they seeing see not; and hearing they hear not, neither do they understand. Verily I say unto you, many prophets and righteous men have desired to see these things which you see, and have not seen them; and to hear those things which you hear, and have not heard them." He instructed his votaries to go not into the way of the Gentiles, warning them, "You shall be brought before governors and kings for my sake, for a testimony against them and the Gentiles."

4

It would be almost out of the question at this late date to get anything like a complete account of what the Nazarene did or taught. There are few still alive who knew him well enough to tender the account, and as is so often the case with religious leaders, those who knew him best are the most unreliable of sources.

He wrote nothing himself; I doubt very much he even knew how to write. And had he known how, he would have felt no need to write anything down: he was that positive the world would end within a very few years. He said, "The time is fulfilled, and the kingdom of God is at hand." And, "There will be some standing here, which shall not taste death till they see the Son of man coming in his kingdom." and, "This generation shall not pass, till all these things be fulfilled."

His disciples have been deterred from writing about their Messiah by this same end-of-the-world assurance. They have always considered it sufficient to rely on their memories for such information about his life and teachings as is necessary until he returns to set up his kingdom.

I believe there can be no reasonable doubt Gestes was the only one who ever recorded any of his words even as they were being spoken. Another of the ironies of religious history! If a life of this Jeshu is ever written and he is made to speak any of his own words (he could easily be made to speak much wiser ones), most of them will have to be culled from among the devastating ridicule and refutations with which Gestes has overwhelmed them in his *Acts and Sayings of Jeshu*, which I brought out some years ago.

As is abundantly proven by the smattering we possess, had we ever so many of his dicta, so ambiguous and contradictory are they, we still could not determine what he believed.

He said, "I and my Father are one." He also said, "My Father is greater than I." He said, "The Father judges no man, but has committed judgment unto the son." But he also said, "I judge no man. And yet if I judge, my judgment is true" and "If any man hear my words, and believe not, I judge him not; for I come not to judge the world, but to save the world" and "For judgment I came into this world, that they which see not might see; and they which see might be made blind."

"Put up again your sword," he said, "...all they that take the sword shall perish with the sword." But then he said, "He that has no sword, let him sell his garment and buy one."

"These things I have spoken unto you," he said, "that in me you might have peace." And, "Think not I am come to send peace on earth," he said; "I come not to send peace but the sword." Also, "Peace I leave with you," he said; "my peace I give unto you." Whereafter he said, "Suppose you that I am come to give peace on earth? I tell you, nay: but rather division."

I have not appended Gestes' comments upon these sayings, Caius, as they are quite lengthy. If you cannot imagine them for yourself, you may read them in *Acts and Sayings of Jeshu*.

All of which goes to show nothing more than that the Nazarene, like all other humans, vacillated between opposing opinions as circumstances dictated.

What is now being promulgated in his name is not the religion of Jeshu but that of Paul of Tarsus. This to anyone who dares look and see is glaringly evinced by the fact Jeshu's personal followers to the man always have and—insofar as they yet live—still do denounce Paul, saying their Master was the Messiah to the Hebrews only and not to the Gentiles with whom Yahweh has not, never has had, and never will have a covenant.

Had it not been for Plato, Socrates would have come down

to us only as a minor character in the works of Xenephon and Aristophanes. Just so, had it not been for Paul, the Nazarene would have fallen into oblivious or vaguely remembered for exactly what he was, a revolutionary personality but withal just another ignorant, deluded, race-prejudiced, Galilean peasant, having neither deserved nor received honors. He is a god only because Paul needed a Messiah, preferably a dead one who did not have, as Gestes would have put it, "the lack of consistency, magnitude, and profundity characteristic of the living," one about whom "to hang the precepts of a new religion, the one and only true religion the world has ever known": his own. Jeshu and his disciples are to Paul and his epistles just what Socrates and Glaucon were to Plato and his dialogues, and just what Gestes, Azzie, Numba, and myself are to this historiette; that is, a semi-fictitious, colorful, and serviceable dramatis personae.

5

Whether I have ever seen this Paul of Tarsus, I am unable to say with any degree of certainty. There probably are not more than three or four years differences in our ages, and, as you know, I too was born on the banks of that most beautiful of all rivers, the Cydnus.

Yet, try as I may, I cannot remember any specific youth whom I can identify as the founder of Christianity. By the way, Caius, if you are not already acquainted with the fact, I might say these followers of Jeshu or Paul are not the first to be called "Christians." The worshipers of the Egyptian bull-god Serapis also bear this name, and his disciples call themselves "the Bishops of Christ." Christ, a name which Jeshu probably never so much as even heard, is the Greek word meaning "the Anointed," and it has been given to Adonis,

Dionysus, and other Hellenic saviors centuries before the time of the Nazarene.

What is more, in their temples here in Rome, I have several times seen Paul's proselytes bowed before images of this same solemn, bearded Serapis, which is labeled "The Christ" and which they mistake for statues of the Nazarene, despite the fact they could not possibly be the likeness of the Jew, of whom no statues are likely to be erected.

Whether I have ever seen Paul, there are in his writings a number of passages—more, a hundred of them at least—which make me feel we did much more in common as striplings than swim in the same waters.

His statement: "My little children, of who I travail in birth again until Christ be formed in you"; his definition of faith: "The substance of things hoped for, the evidence of things not seen"; and his assurance to the Galatians: "For as many of you as have been baptized unto Christ have put on Christ"; what surmises these telltale Lingam-Yoni tidbits inspire in an erstwhile Tarsus rowdy! In his *Epistle to the Romans*, Paul speaks of the sins he once committed. In a number of places he, "Glorifying in 'His infirmities,'" finds a morbid, religious delight in suffering from an unnamed malady. As he so euphemistically puts it: "a thorn is the flesh, the messenger of Satan to buffet me."

I know nothing certain about either these sins or this so-carefully-unnamed disease, but linking his repeated mentions of them with what I do know of particular ceremonies of which these aforementioned quotations are echoes both in idea and phraseology, I draw conclusions sufficient to plunge me into some very pleasant reminiscences.

At the beginning of this story I spoke—in connection with making Gestes' acquaintance—of my recounting an experience I once had on the banks of the immemorial Cydnus. I was only about 17 years old then, but another 49 years would not dim my memory of that day.

I was lying under a tree beside the river one afternoon, when I saw a nude girl coming upstream along the opposite bank. I could hear her calling, but since she was some distance away I was unable to hear what she said. I watched, wondering just what she was about. My initial suspicion was that she was a wench brought out there for the pleasure of some optimistic youth who, having found her a disappointment, had run off with her clothes as a compensatory merriment. But as she drew nearer, I was able to see the rather beautiful roundness of her face and the decidedly beautiful roundness of her breasts, and I immediately renounced my conjecture.

Moreover, I could by then distinguish her words, which went something like this: "Shaddus of Shaddus, accept my maidenhead."

Readily concluding Shaddus must be a god, since no mortal would have been so unresponsive to such supplications, I stripped off my clothes, slipped into the water, pushed away from the bank under the surface, and swam as nearly as I could across to where she was.

Recalling this event I have often wondered if I am not the father of a divinely conceived and virgin-born offspring, for it was divine and she was a virgin. In which case, I also wonder if his paternal inheritance has been of sufficient potency to offset the taint of godliness and bring him through to manliness.

It would be just preposterous enough to constitute a major chapter in the story of *Great Faiths* should some prying, atheist historian get himself thrown to the lions for proving that all my books against Jeshu and other saviors were designed and executed with the intent to clear all grounds for the universal religious acceptance of my own deified bastard.

CHAPTER VIII

The Possessed

1

One day, after arising from Numba's table, Gestes became violently ill. A cold sweat broke out on his body, and wrenching cramps seized his internals. Suffering considerably and fearing for his life, he asked the centurion to ride in haste to Tiberias and get a physician.

Numba demurred, contending that drugs could be of no avail since it was evident Gestes had fallen under the spell of evil spirits. He proposed, instead of a physician, to sacrifice an unblemished lamb and to offer up their united prayers beseeching God to deliver the patient from the clutches of the Devil and his legions.

Gestes, to whom this was abject stupidity, so insisted upon having medical aid that Numba eventually relented and, downcast, left the house.

2

Having endured his misery as best he could for more than the time it should have taken Numba to make the journey to and from Tiberias, Gestes called Numba's wife and asked her to look and see if the physician was in sight.

She reddened with embarrassment and finally confessed that her husband had not gone to the city of Herod but, learning that the healing prophet Jeshu of Nazareth was nearby, had gone to seek him instead.

Enraged, Gestes leaped from his bed. So vehemently did he curse the centurion and the prophet that he strangled upon his curses and vomited. Purging his stomach in this manner rid him of the poison which afflicted him and brought him relief. He cursed a while longer, then returned to his couch and fell asleep.

3

When the centurion returned home some time later and saw Gestes peacefully sleeping, he was almost beside himself with exultation and self-esteem.

He had, it seems, located the Nazarene and made known his mission. Jeshu, urged by his followers, many of whom knew Numba as the donor of their tabernacle in Magdala, had agreed to accompany him back to the house to see what could be done. However, the centurion, afraid to let Gestes know of his actions until sure of their success, deterred the healer. "Lord," he said, "it is some distance to where I live. The sick man might die before we arrive. Moreover, I am not worthy that you should make this trip for my sake. Nor is it necessary that you make it: only say the word and my servant will be instantly cured."

This act of faith had merited the dullard a compliment of which he was childishly proud. "Verily, I have nowhere else encountered such great faith, no not in all Israel."

Numba—obviously ready to take up his stand on the right hand of God—could not resist the temptation to awaken Gestes and tell him of this compliment and of the miracle to which they owed his recovery. When Gestes had heard Numba's tale, he could not resist the temptation to throw up to the centurion the vile truth and complexion of his unheavenly healing.

Once under way, he continued until he had told the centurion all the degrading opinions he had formed of him. Which, it is hardly necessary to say, cost Gestes his position.

CHAPTER IX

The Making of a Mountebank

1

After being discharged by Marcus Numba, Gestes was once more in need of an income. This time, however, chance was less willing to come to his rescue.

He was not dismayed. Few men felt less in need of chance than Gestes Demias. He had a phenomenal intellect and put great faith in it as a trustworthy provider.

Moving back to his cottage in Tiberias, he began working at odd jobs. To whatever purpose he put his hand, he learned something. Since it offered almost unlimited opportunities to indulge his somewhat roguish inclinations, Gestes took particular pleasure in "trading," and in his happiness all who knew him found a share.

I repeat it, Caius, you would have valued being acquainted with this man. Both mentally and physically, he was a throwback to the brightest days of Athens.

2

One day, about four or maybe five months after beginning his career as a merchant Gestes rushed up to me as I lay upon my couch in camp and told me he was the bearer of good news.

"Tell me about it," I said.

"Business brought me over to Magdala day-before-yesterday," he began, "and who should I run into but Jeshu, my ancient enemy. He was speaking before an assemblage of his devotees. It is close to the time of the Jewish Passover, and he is even now on his way to Jerusalem. He had stopped in Magdala to bid farewell to some of his followers.

"My life-long interest in gods got the upper hand of me and demanded I stop to hear him once again. It seems he is suffering considerably these days from professional jealousy. He spoke almost exclusively of the marvels to be performed by 'false messiahs' who, according to his predictions, will imitate him in days to come.

"While listening to his counsels against believing any of these impostors," Gestes chuckled, "I gave virgin birth to an idea."

"And what was the nature of your mental offspring?" I asked.

"It was a mongrel at birth," he explained. "I have been all this time trying to figure out just what it was. This afternoon, much to the betterment of our financial prospects, I figured it out. I have decided to become a 'false messiah,' a heaven sent physician, a practitioner of applied theology, demonology, and certain other first class ologies.

"Having studied diligently for years, I have mastered practically the whole of the magical pharmacopoeia. I have learned the art of exorcism from the Essenes of Qumran; the ways of occultism from the Magi of Persia; the science of stargazing from the astrologers of Abydos, Sais and Memphis; the secrets of the Assyrian sorcerers and mystagogues; the knowledge contained in the *Solonic Book of Remedies;* yes, and the wisdom of the Zend-Avesta.

"I am versed in the *Sepher-Yetzirah*, in the magic papyri of the Greeks, and in the Cabala. The Cabala was handed down from Adam to Moses and from Moses to a fortunate few of this day, and is all-inclusive in its treatment of theurgy or white magic, which is the science of inveigling divine powers to do your will, and goety, black magic, or necromancy, which is commerce with the legions of the damned. Above all, prompted by my reading in the *Book of Tobit*, the story of the demon Asmodeus, who did countless evil deeds in Palestine before Tobias, who, instructed to do so by the angel Raphael, burned the heart and liver of a fish caught from the Tigris, the smell of which drove Asmodeus from the land. I have sought and discovered the olfactory likes and dislikes of the spirits of unclean blood, of blindness, of fever, of witchcraft—in short, of all ailments or noncompletions—superstitions and stupidities being the only exceptions. I have likewise ascertained the stories of all known demons, specters, ghosts, vampires, necrophilic beings, and their innumerable kin. I have... What all have I done?

"I don't know myself the extent of my portentous knowledge. But I will after an hour's stock taking. I'm a bit excited just now by my prospects."

"To what purpose have you put forth all this intellectual labor?" I inquired.

"I'm surprised some other medicaster has not thought of it long ago," he marveled. "I'm going to Jerusalem, and you are going with me. Get leave from your camp for a month, and be sure to bring with you everything you own, everything you can buy, steal, or borrow which will declare you a Roman soldier.

"I'm going to concoct a salve that will cure a Hebrew's ills. Yes, and those of a lot of other deluded fools as well. When smeared over the body, my potion will give off an absolutely unbearable stink that is fatal to all demons, devils, evil spirits, and, in short, the nightmarish chimeras of religious fears, rites, and superstitions."

"And how about the man that uses it?" I asked.

"It isn't my primary intent to kill him also, but if I do... Well, that may well be the best quality of my ointment. Anyone who has no more sense than to believe what I will say to sell it ought to be killed for buying it.

"Of course, one application will not suffice to kill the purchaser or chase away the demons. Oh no, we're not going to let anyone disprove us that quickly. You see, due to the greater purity of the air up here, or possibly to the change of climate, these nasty nether world inhabitants have the power to hold their breath for a week or ten days. I believe we can glut our passions in that time, and still have enough left to get us out of the country. Are you following me?"

"I'm very much afraid that I am," I admitted a bit reluctantly.

"What?" he asked. "You're not going squeamish on me? I'll agree the element of beauty is somewhat lacking in my plans. It generally is where money-making is involved. But if I must justify such unjustifiable actions, I will do my best.

"Since the time of the Jewish Passover is at hand, the Children of Israel are flocking to Jerusalem like the sheep they are.

"Whether they are aware of it or not, they are gathering there for the sole purpose of getting themselves fleeced. Hundreds of thousands of these poor devils have half starved themselves, their women, and their children that they might have a few half-shekels for this momentous occasion. I trust you know these Jews well enough already to accept this premise without further proof. Now, if we don't get their money, a crew of pot-gutted priests will. If you don't accept this premise already, you will once you get to Jerusalem and have a look at the Jewish temple, one of the largest store-houses and the largest slaughter house in the whole world. You will see hundreds of corpulent, god-chosen butchers (otherwise known as priests) lifting their holy finery as they step over steaming entrails or wade through rivulets of the blood of sacrificial animals in their ministerial functions of receiving still more animals and tributes of countless other varieties.

"Now, if we get the peasants' money, our clients will get a good lesson in credulity. Whereas, if the sacredotal parasites get it, their simple-minded hosts will be duped the same way the same time next year, and the year after that, and the year after that.

"I'll grant you that to cheat a lot of poor imbeciles out of their meager savings is wrong, grievously wrong. But we must view this thing in its greater as well as its lesser context. All we are going to do, when all is said and done, is cheat other cheaters out of their opportunities to cheat.

"I would like to see my irreligious convictions profusely copied and distributed throughout the Empire. To realize this, I need money, quite a sum of money. With my share of what we make out of this project, I am going to bring out some books that, for a happy few at least, will make impossible the future perpetration of just such swindles as had made them possible."

3

The setting sun that evening found Gestes, Lais, and I perched upon swaying camels and heading for Jerusalem.

CHAPTER X

Rogue's Harvest

1

If you have never attended Passover in Jerusalem, it is almost impossible to visualize such a throng as attends them. I have heard it said that as many as three million pilgrims gather for the observance of this feast. Having seen one, I cannot bring myself to doubt the assertion. Great tidal waves of human beings surge along the narrow streets and clog the alleyways.

By the time we reached Jerusalem, there was not a house of any description to be let. Not even a stable could we rent in which to mix our wonder-working salve. We had to pay an exorbitant price for four dilapidated walls, the only space that we could find that was remotely suitable as a workshop.

To secure a room for Lais, we were compelled to return to a little village called Bethpage, almost two miles from the city, and even there she had to accept lodging in the squalid shack of a poverty stricken Jewish family, and at a price the tattered landlord no doubt gloated over to his dying day.

Knowing we would be unable to leave our work long enough during the coming days to visit her, Gestes bought a mare ass and its colt for Lais so she might ride in to see us and take back such purchases as she saw fit to make. Princess that she was, Lais accepted these makeshift accommodations in characteristic good spirits, asked us to have no further worries about her but to hasten back to the holy city and start relieving sufferers of their ills and money.

2

Back in Jerusalem, we made our way to the marketplace, passing through congested streets some of whose arcades, alleys, and intersections were arbored over with palm and willow branches to represent desert abodes in commemoration of the Israelites' years of wandering after the much-belied escape from Egypt.

The marketplace itself was pandemonium, an unforgettable admixture of all the good, the bad, the worst and the best of practically everything humanity has to display. The dregs of human degeneracy were everywhere so numerous and so conspicuous as to almost monopolize the scene. Wasted, stooped, and crooked men and women, many with cataracts on their eyes and livid boils on their faces and necks, walked or dragged themselves about, often accompanied by a litter of their young. Everywhere, we saw cripples, paralytics, lepers, consumptives, and drooling idiots. Filthy beggars swarmed about crying their self-pity and, with a technique acquired through long years of competitive effort, if not by actual congenital conditioning, displaying their deformities in the hope of receiving alms.

Viewing this aggregation of human derelicts, their withered limbs and distorted trunks twisted into nightmarish grotesques, parts of their anatomies already dead and mummified, other parts dying and emitting an unbearable stench, Gestes offered this comment: "It is my opinion, Servilius, that every person should have at least one look at such a spectacle as this;

it might go far toward ridding humanity of its unreasoned attachment to the fetish of life."

Most of all, Gestes and I studied the craftsmen, our soon-to-be rivals. Throngs of them, each wearing something to designate his trade, were there. In the outer court of the temple, Moneychangers, each with a denarius dangling from one ear, bartered the unadorned half-shekel required in the Sacred Tribute in exchange for image bearing pagan coins, since priests were forbidden to take foreign coins because their holy writ is very explicit in its denunciation of graven images.

In stalls beyond the temple walls, seamstresses flaunted threaded needles of great size. Perfumers wore girdles decked with phials of ointments or flasks of scented herbs. Fruit sellers milled about with baskets filled with citrons, dates, pears, and pomegranates, each proclaiming the superiority of his wares. Thieves filtered through the crowds like a cleansing tide, washing away everything of value not firmly secured.

Clamorously eager, bird-vendors offered for sale the small birds required for various sacrifices, especially doves or pigeons. Herders minded bleating sheep and goats, bellowing bullocks and braying asses.

Rival merchants swore to the quality of wines made from wheat, from the dates of Jericho, or from the grapes of Engedi. Contending noises made hearing all but impossible.

The smell of diseased, unclean and sweating bodies, of fresh fallen dung, of rancid breath, and of burning incense mingled with unguents, perfumes, the oblations of virgin myrrh, galbanum, Saban frankincense, and the tallow vapor of the thirteen bulls slaughtered for the Grand Sacrifice.

We weighed all these phenomena in their relation to our enterprise and, being well pleased, set about our business. We brought a great number of small earthen vessels, hurried up to our workshop and began to mix and jar our malodorous catholicon.

3

The next morning we arose early and made our final preparations for the day.

Gestes stained his skin to a dusky olive hue, powdered his hair, and put on a long gray beard. He dressed himself in an all-inclusive assortment of rags and fineries. Zealots, Essenes, Nasaraei, Hemerobaptists, Magi, and the members of all brotherhoods or factions could have found something in his attire which acclaimed him a compeer. He carried a staff and looked very much like a Hebrew prophet.

For myself, as a Roman guardsman, I wore everything from a leather tunic to *lorica segmentats*, from regulation sandals to *gladius ibericus*, *focale*, and beplumed helmet. I even put a long knife in my *cingulum militare* for good measure in the event I should need it to arm Gestes or should I need help in an exigency.

I helped him carry a small booth we had constructed during the night, together with a supply of our salve, until we reached the entrance to the court of the Gentiles, and there I heaped the whole upon Gestes and followed at a distance.

Although it was scarcely daybreak, and the gates had just opened, the most advantageous positions were already occupied. Gestes, undaunted, sought out the one he most wanted and began to plant his booth on top of the one already there. Remember, we were among Jews, and Jewish tradesmen at that, so you can imagine for yourself what followed.

The original tenant, his arms gyrating before him, his splayed fingers writhing like so many snakes, came at Gestes on the waves of a veritable flood of abuses and protests. Fearing not at all for his life, but greatly for his artificial beard, Gestes retreated behind the two booths and tried manfully to oppose in kind the avalanche of words.

As he circled about, he pulled the Hebrew's booth out of place and even overturned it. A considerable audience began to gather around the contestants.

I waited a moment, then drew my sword and parted the rabble, planting myself between the two antagonists. As a Roman guardsman, I demanded an explanation for their breach of peace and quiet. Both began vociferous accusations. Bystanders joined in with their testimonials, most of which favored the Jew.

Silencing the others by threatening to call down upon them my fellow Romans, I listened for a while to the charges of the two claimants, cursed each for his unseemly conduct and ended by forcing the Israelite to move to a new locality.

This over with, Gestes put our booth in order, while I returned to our workshop and changed my clothes to those more fitting a partner in the enterprise.

4

Gestes did the selling. I mixed the vile-smelling ingredients which went into our wonder-salve and kept him supplied. Ah, you should have seen Gestes at his bargaining, Caius. It was a revelation. He was a good spokesman and a shrewd salesman.

Never, I believe, did a people's superstitions serve better to loose their purse strings than they did that day. The amount of money he took in, remembering it was mostly in small coins, was all but unbelievable.

Cripples forgot their twisted trunks and withered limbs, beggars their valetudinary bodies and pus-filled eyes. All manner of human dregs who for months had saved their alms or earnings in order to buy sparrows, white pigeons, unblemished lambs, or even fatted bullocks to offer as sacrifices, forgot those things when they heard Gestes, and bought earthen jars of a stinking paste in their stead.

Nor were unfortunates the only ones to purchase our wares. Sailors, farmers, toilers, merchants, housewives, fellow swindlers, dignitaries—Gestes ensnared them all with his ambiguous, insinuating references to occult powers, netherworld affiliations, sacred books, and foreign, polysyllabically named necromancers, prestidigitators, and theurgists.

CHAPTER XI

The Widow's Mite

1

Lais visited us shortly before noon and, to our surprise, almost decimated our scheme. Seeing us defraud such obviously needy simpletons as so many of our customers were, she let her emotions override her reason. The pathetic hopefulness in which these wretches parted with their meager savings upset her. Although she had been warned beforehand and won over to our views, although she had all but sworn to exercise self-control, when she was confronted with the outlay in its sordid reality, her effeminate benignity revolted completely.

To make things still worse, a slatternly hag who for some time had vacillated between our booth and that of a bird vendor, seeing the beautiful and well-dressed Lais talking with us in such seriousness, was finally resolved to buy our salve. With the look of a tired mule deeply embedded in her bloated, pock-marked face, she humbly sidled up to Gestes bearing in her arms a pitiable, fleshless infant with eyes irretrievably despoiled by vermin and infection.

"Please, good man," she began, speaking through thick lips whose muscular structure had given away, allowing the lower one to sag like a camel's, displaying, in lieu of teeth, jagged rows of brown decay. "I haven't enough money to buy a full portion of your salve but, please, for my poor, fatherless child's sake, won't you accept a poor widow's last mite for just a pinch of your wonderful salve? God will make it up to you; I know he will. Won't you, Mister? Please."

The bird vendor across from us, seeing he was losing the sale of a sacrificial sparrow, began to revile our wares, our tactics, and our persons for the thousandth time that morning. Gestes' eyes narrowed. His jaw set. He handed the woman a jar of paste and received her money, dropping it with revulsion into our money box. Lais groaned.

"Stay here," said Gestes, turning to me with unseeing eyes. He put an arm about the almost inert body of Lais and led her away.

Some moments later he returned alone, silently took a handful of the larger coins from our profits, crossed over to a perfumer's stall and purchased an expensive alabaster box of spikenard. Still without meeting my questioning gaze, he disappeared again.

2

It was some time before Gestes reappeared. When he did, he dismissed the sorry incident, saying, "Thank the gods that's over." He elbowed me away from the booth with a slighting remark about the woeful decrease in business during his absence and straightaway began to call with gusto the merits of our demon-dispelling febrifuge. Nothing else of an especially disconcerting nature interrupted us thereafter.

Gestes bargained as if with a vengeance. Time after time I had to go find more earthen jars, mix more paste, and replenish his supply. What a day!

That night we were so tired, both of us fell asleep while discussing preparations for the morrow.

CHAPTER XII

Disaster

1

The next morning our claim to an auspicious business location was contested with all but fatal consequences.

Suspecting we would endeavor to reenact the high-handed farce of the previous day, several merchants whose trade had greatly suffered because of Gestes' proficiency, banded together to bring about his undoing. Foreseeing something like this, we took all due precautions. Gestes once more carried his prophet's staff and I my Iberic sword and long knife.

When we reached the temple precincts, I went ahead to reconnoiter. Five Jews and yesterday's tenant were gathered about the tenant's booth, which stood in the space where our booth had been the day before. Each of the six was armed with a shepherd's crook, the most effective weapon they could carry without incurring the suspicion of Roman guardsmen.

But, and this had been our greatest worry, although soldiers stood or walked nearby, none of them seemed in any way affiliated with our rivals. With a Hebrew's characteristic mistrust of Roman authority, the six had taken it upon themselves to deal with us in their own rights.

I hurried back to Gestes. Taking up our belongings, he made his way to the favored spot. Arriving there, he purposely stumbled, lost his balance and plunged headlong, directing the load upon his back into the intruding stall and with the same movement, swinging his staff to land a blow full upon the tenant's shin. The two booths, with their mingled contents, went crashing to the ground.

The tenant rolled in agony amid the wreckage. The other merchants, seeing Gestes go down beneath his burden, sprang forward with all the gusto of accidentally victorious cowards. Gestes, in falling, had made it a point to execute a sideways somersault. He came to a position half sitting, half kneeling, in time to meet the foremost assailant with a blow which, since we were resolved to have no casualties, was almost too well aimed. It caught a man just above the left ear, causing him to collapse like an empty water skin.

Running up behind him, I eliminated one of our opponents with a resonant slap across the buttocks with the flat of my sword. Turning and seeing my weapon, this witling must have attributed the stinging of his fundament to a lacerating wound. He gathered his posterior into his hands and vanished among the crowd frantically announcing his impending death.

In the meantime, Gestes received a blow upon the head which momentarily flattened him out upon the ground, unconscious and unprotected. Shoving the fellow closest to me and sending him sprawling over, I moved to shield Gestes. I glanced down at my sword to make sure it was crosswise before using it upon our two remaining enemies. When I looked up, the two had almost disappeared into the arms of a gigantic Lycian guardsman.

My face must have bespoke my astonishment at his bulk. He stood there, a behelmeted mountain of human flesh, and grinned like a seven-year-old boy. "If those two don't make you a good meal," I managed to say, "there are three others here you may have for the asking." To this, the behemoth grunted good-naturedly, but made no answer. Seeing thereby that he did not understand Latin, I asked: "And how about Hebrew?"

As a chance answer to this, he extended to me his two captives. Knowing their hostility would remain at low tide so long as this incarnate Mars was about, I accepted the offer.

"Now," I told them, "get your rubbish, human and otherwise, and clear out before I tell Samson here you're a bunch of Philistines." Without a word of protest, they followed instructions.

2

Once this fracas was over and Gestes was, despite several ugly bruises, his old self again, we put our booth in order and settled down anew to a monetary harvest.

Having learned much the day before, Gestes did his negotiating with increased efficiency. I began to have considerable difficulty in finding earthen jars of a size and shape to serve our purpose. Before the morning was half over, we had to start selling our demon-chaser spread on strips of wood. The stink of this salve was fast coming to rival those of Jewish beggars, animal dung, and the temple slaughter blocks or sacrificial altars.

The day was at its prime. I returned from our workshop with a new mixing of salve. Gestes had completely sold out his supply in my absence and was impatient to recommence vending. Throwing down my load, I was hastily slashing it into small squares when a great commotion broke out behind me. Too busy to look up, I contented myself with wondering what it was all about. Then something hit me on the back of the head and upset me into our stinking paste.

Angrily springing to my feet, I barely managed to sidestep

a frantically fleeing ass. Reestablishing my upright position, I quickly looked about to ascertain what was being enacted. About ten paces away and heading directly for our booth was the Nazarene.

Like one gone violently mad, he was striking out right and left with a long, makeshift whip, upending bird cages, kicking over money benches, shouldering aside fruit baskets and wineskins, and upsetting anything else upon which he chanced to come. Such people as were not standing in opened-mouth bewilderment were dementedly scampering about, weeping in their consternation, or cursing in their wrath.

Fowls began to infest the air like winged demons. Cattle, sheep, goats, and asses took fright and ran amok. The whole courtyard was converted into a shrieking, teeming pit of rage and panic. Catching up the knife with which I had been cubing our salve, I started toward the Jew, intent upon ridding the world once and for all of his meddlesome presence.

Gestes, however, conceiving the same idea at almost the same instant, grabbed my arm and wrenched the weapon from my grasp, then ran to do the thing himself. Confronting his enemy, he seized him by the throat, but, just as he was about to deliver the fatal blow, a maddened bullock caught him upon its horns and hurled him insensible across the wreckage of a fallen booth.

Springing forward, I landed a crushing blow to the Nazarene's jaw, hoping thereby to stay him until I could recover my knife. It had landed among some bird cages, and I was some time in extracting it. Once I had done so, I started to return to the fray, but cattle were bolting past in such numbers and with such reckless terror, I had to abandon my purpose, grab Gestes from beneath their trampling hooves, and drag him to safety outside the Temple court.

3

As soon as I had Gestes out of danger and was sure he was neither dead nor dying, I ran back to the court, hoping to retrieve all or some portion of our money.

One look at the swarms of beggars crawling over the wreckage and squabbling among crushed fruits and animal excrement sufficed to dissuade me. I turned and hurried back to Gestes. Lifting him upon my shoulder, I carried him as gently and as speedily as I could up to our workshop.

Trying to find a physician in that city of feasting and turmoil would be more than useless, so I administered to him myself, bathing and binding up his wounds and, insofar as I knew, easing his discomfort. His wounds were very painful but not gravely serious. A short horn had pierced his right hip, and something had struck him across the face in such a way that both his eyes were swollen tight.

It was dark before I was able to bring him back to consciousness. Even then his mind was far from being right. He made irrelevant answers to my inquiries and was almost puerile in his repeated supplications to and for Lais.

I couldn't keep from wondering myself what she would have thought and done if, coming to the market place, she found it in ruins and we were not about. I very much doubted that she had ridden in that day following her unhappy first visit. Then, too, she knew where our workshop was, and I reasoned that if she missed us at the Temple, she would assuredly have sought us there.

I endeavored to quiet Gestes with this line of reasoning and succeeded to the extant that eventually he fell into a troubled sleep.

CHAPTER XIII

Lais

1

By daybreak, Gestes was feeling somewhat better. His head was cleared, and he was able to advise me in my feeble efforts to substitute for a physician. The wound in his hip still throbbed painfully but by no means so excruciatingly as during the night. His eyes, although they remained swollen shut throughout the day, continued to show a gradual improvement.

He was still worried about Lais. She had been quite shaken up at the sight of our ignominious trading and Gestes had only partially succeeded in allaying her repugnance. I tried once more to reason him out of his misgivings, although I was myself growing increasingly uneasy.

2

Late that afternoon, since Lais had neither made an appearance nor sent us any message, I left Gestes to care for his own needs as best he could and went to Bethpage to see what was detaining her. The aged landlord greeted me when I arrived and, in response to my request to see her, said Lais had gone with his daughter for a twilight ride.

I was suspicious, detecting an element of deceit in his story, but not having time to wait and still get back to Jerusalem before the gates closed for the night, I did not press the old man. Instead, asking him to tell Lais of my visit and instruct her to come to our workshop the next day, I took my leave.

Gestes was somewhat distraught by the outcome of my visit to Bethpage, but nothing could be done, so he forcibly forgot his fears in order to get a much needed night's rest.

3

The next day dragged itself out interminably. With a moment by moment increase in both our expectations and disappointment, we waited hour after hour for Lais to arrive.

Not even the opening of Gestes' eyes early that morning was sufficient to stay our sinking spirits. By mid-afternoon our fears had overcome our hopes, and although Gestes could walk only at the price of great pain, he would not consent to remain behind. And so I went out and hired a boy and an ass to help me get him to Bethpage.

It was a slow and tedious journey. Gestes rode until he could no longer bear to do so, then he dismounted to walk a short distance and stretch out upon the ground for a few minutes' rest. The boy and I stayed at his side and tried in every way we could think of to lessen his sufferings.

It was almost dark when we finally reached our destination. This time it was obvious by the way the old Jew hid behind the half-opened door that something was wrong. With ominously drooped shoulders and shaking hands, the ancient peered out at us as if expecting to be assaulted. "It was through no fault of mine," he said. "She did it of her own accord, although I think she was bewitched."

"What are you talking about?" asked Gestes hoarsely.

"It was an impostor, Jeshu of Nazareth, who did it."

"Did what? Where is she?" Gestes pushed his way inside and started to look around.

"She is gone," the Jew said, spreading wide his arms.

"What happened? Tell me everything," Gestes demanded.

"It started just after her visit with you in Jerusalem last Sunday," the old man said, hobbling into the courtyard and away from Gestes, who followed fast on his heels. "When she got back, she tied her mare to that post and came into the house. A few moments later two men came and took the colt that was leashed beside its mother. I asked by whose permission they were taking it. One said: 'The Lord has need of him.' Thinking that by 'Lord,' he meant one of you, I let him go. But a moment later, I grew suspicious, so I ran in the house and asked your woman. She confirmed that it was a theft, and we ran back out together and followed the men. By the time we caught up with them, they had joined the party of this false prophet, Jeshu. I understand you have encountered him before."

"Yes, go on," Gestes urged him. "What happened to Lais?"

"I can't say for certain. There was a great multitude, much noise and confusion. We listened to Jeshu's mad talk for a while. What he said was of no consequence, save that your woman seemed to believe it. She allowed him to depart for Jerusalem on the colt. After that she seemed troubled in her mind, possessed of demons in my opinion."

The old man raised a trembling hand and pointed at me. "When she saw you coming yesterday, she asked me to tell you she was out walking, or rather riding. She said she was not sure just what to do and wanted more time to think. Today, she took a beautiful alabaster box of spikenard and, I am told, went to this Jeshu at Bethany where he dined in the house of Simon the Pharisee. Breaking open the box, she poured its contents over the mountebank's head and feet. They say she even dried his feet with her beautiful hair."

Stunned, Gestes sank to the ground. The old man took heart to finish his story. "Coming back afterwards, she got her things and left. She gave me this for the one of you who is Gestes." From his tattered cloak he brought forth a rolled letter. I read it after Gestes had finished.

She said we had misunderstood the Nazarene; that he was indeed the Messiah, Son of the one and only God, *Adonai*. She expressed great regrets at leaving Gestes without first talking with him, but said she was afraid just then to see him. She promised, however, to return some day and try to show him wherein she had acted wisely.

For his consideration in her absence, she closed her letter with this question: "Granting, Gestes, that practically every significant incident and practically every doctrine, both in the life and teachings of Jeshu and in the history and teachings of the sacred books of my people, is echoed in the mythology or philosophy of unbelieving nations, does this not only prove that the Devil, having heard the prophets foretell the coming of the Son of God, has set about causing the heathens to acclaim many of their heroes and kings to be the sons of Jove or other so-called deities? Is it not clear that Satan's object in this is to lead men to imagine the true history of Jeshu is one with these pagan parallels?"

After he had finished reading the letter, Gestes handed it to me and, without a word, limped away into the gathering dusk. Knowing that such things are best borne alone, when I in turn had finished the letter, I went into the house, threw myself upon Lais' bed and, weighed down by accumulating disasters, fell into a deep sleep.

CHAPTER XIV

The Search

1

Toward dawn I awoke, and, to my dismay, I found Gestes had not yet come in. Jumping up, I ran out to look for him, uneasy lest it was his wound more than his sorrow which detained him.

It was not dark. A full moon on the western horizon illuminated the ground, and I searched everywhere I could think of that he might have taken refuge. All in vain! I could discover no trace of him. A new fear then presented itself. What if his grief had caused him to resolve upon some mad revenge? I redoubled my efforts.

Morning came and went, still I sought but gained no clue to Gestes' whereabouts. In the early afternoon, I learned where the Nazarene and his followers were. I hurried there hoping to arrive before Gestes did, should his vengeance take that course.

The Jew, as usual, was talking, and a group of people crowded around to hear what he said. I passed among these to ascertain whether or not either Gestes or Lais was there. Neither was present, but, afraid to leave lest Gestes might appear, I stayed about for some time.

While I waited, having nothing else to do, I listened. As I

have said, the Nazarene was a pleasant and impressive speaker.

What a name this man would have made for himself among the Sophists! Never, I believe, did another human make absurdities so attractive, so seemingly plausible.

I remember having a thought concerning one element of his counsel. "Should men of wealth and power, should Tiberius himself hear these dicta, your cult would not stand in want of the financial and political support of the whole Roman world."

Ironically enough, this observation was called forth by the supposed consolation he offered to the impoverished, the injured, and the enslaved. He said, oh, so soothingly: "You who toil, obey your masters, and be worthy of your hire. Be proud of and content with your lowly positions. Seek not after worldly things, but lay up riches in Heaven. Love your enemies of high estate. Pity them, for it is harder for a rich man to enter into Heaven than for a camel to crawl through that small gate in Jerusalem's walls that is known as the 'Needle's Eye.' Kiss the foot that grinds you into the earth, for yours is the cream of the afterlife. If by theft, burdensome taxation, or unjust claims any man should take your grain, give him your livestock also."

What a thief's paradise he would make of this earth! What irresistible incentives he offers one to become his neighbor's enemy, his oppressor, a forger of unjust claims!

I have no doubt whatsoever, Caius, if these Christians would follow their Messiah's teachings and content themselves with the provinces, Rome would be only too glad to make theirs the out-of-state religion. Unfortunately, ignorance is evangelistic. But we won't go into that. I'm trying to bring this story to a close.

2

I finally gave up hoping to find Gestes coming after the Nazarene. Or perhaps I should say, other fears overpowered those I had previously held.

At any rate, I left the messianic group and, after going once more to look for Gestes in Lais' room, went to Jerusalem. Here I continued my quest until well on into the night. At last fatigue and disappointment so overcame me, I decided to give up and rest.

On my way to our workshop where I proposed to sleep until morning, I passed through a garden and almost stumbled over a sleeping man. Despite a total lack of similarity between the two men or their garments, my fancy led me to believe for a moment that I had found Gestes where exhaustion had felled him as he tried to reach our roofless walls.

I was disillusioned of course when I saw the sleeper's moonlit face. Stepping quickly back, I was in the act of making an embarrassed retreat when suspicion stayed me in my tracks. Without having derived any definite idea to whom they belonged, I was suddenly positive I was acquainted with those features.

I leaned over to scrutinize them anew. Sure enough, here was one of the fishermen with whom Gestes and I had conversed that day in Galilee before our first meeting with the Nazarene. Looking around, I saw other men lying here and there. Thinking Jeshu might be among them, I stole from one sleeper to the next, my knife drawn, resolved upon murdering the Nazarene while he slumbered. However, he was not among them. All my disappointments, which for the moment had been lifted by this dread resolve, fell upon me again with a crushing weight.

I dragged myself to our ruined abode, pulled off my clothes, wrapped a sheet about me, and plunged into a deep sleep.

CHAPTER XV

In the Early Morning

1

Long before sunup the next morning, I was awakened by the barking of what must have been every watchdog at every cot and sheepfold on the whole of the Mount of Olives.

Jumbled shouts reached me from the garden below. Although the voices were plainly audible, I tried in vain to grasp the exact words being spoken. Jumping up, I ran outside to see what was going on.

Men were darting here and there among the trees that stood at the bottom of the garden. Some carried torches, and by their torchlight I could see that at least a few of them were Roman soldiers. Still I could not gather enough from their shouts to ascertain the cause or meaning of it all.

Drawing my sheet closer about me—there was a cold breeze and I had on no clothes—I hurried down to investigate. Scarcely was I under way when someone leaped out from behind a tree, seized me in his arms, and began to call to his companions. "Here is one of them! I've caught one of them."

Reasoning I could easily prove my identity and innocence should I be taken up for trial, I was not frightened, at least not at first. But when another fellow came running my way and shouted, "Crucify him along with his 'King of the Jews,' " I began to have considerable misgivings.

Since this "King of the Jews" accusation sounded very much like treason, and since men found guilty of treason, by Roman law, are decapitated, this man's instruction to "crucify" me could have but one meaning: I was in the hands of the mob. It is characteristic of a mob to execute its victim and inquire later concerning his innocence or guilt.

Just then, farther down the incline, I caught a glimpse of the Nazarene. He had upon each arm, like giant leeches, Sadducean priests. Everything was suddenly made plain to me. Jeshu had been seized, most likely for having wrecked the stalls and thereby indirectly robbing the temple of a few half-shekels in revenue. The proffered charge of treason was no doubt based upon his claim of being the Messiah, but his real crime, the just punishment for which would in no wise serve to glut the priests' insatiable appetite for revenge, was that he had desecrated their most holy precincts, the hidden holy of holies, the sacred treasury.

The destroyer was now himself to be destroyed! Believe it, Caius, even under circumstances that personally threatened me, this revelation caused my heart to leap for joy. With an effort augmented by this happy disclosure, by a simultaneous forward lunge and twisting of my shoulders, I sent my captor sprawling upon the grass some feet away.

The other, who had just arrived, grabbed at me but only succeeded in fastening his hold upon my sheet. Slipping out of this, I bounded across the garden stark naked, evaded others who would have retaken me, and made good my escape.

2

Once back in the roofless workshop, I pulled my clothes on and sat down to think. The Nazarene was out of the way at last. Of this I was certain. If saved from mob violence by the few Romans present, he still had no chance to escape. The Passover must have its annual Bar Abbas! *Yahweh* must have his feast of blood, human blood! In Moses' time, the blood of Egyptian first-born and the animal blood smeared on doorposts to protect the Hebrews. Who could now serve better than this Galilean, a self-appointed Bar Abbas, Son of the Father? But Romans will not tolerate the death penalty as a punishment for offenses against the gods or the priesthood. Therefore, the charge of treason. Jeshu had long allowed himself to be called the Messiah, and to be a Messiah was to be a traitor to Rome. As for Pontius Pilate, one Jew more or less, what did it matter to him?

A great sense of relief spread over me. "Another of the ironies of religion," I mused. "Ambitious as an atoning savior, the Nazarene is to die for treason, not for the transgressions of others." I leaned back upon my makeshift bed and sighed aloud. "If only I were assured of Gestes' safety, I believe I could stretch out and sleep for a solid week."

With what bitter mockery this thought was brought back to me a short while later when a boy approached to announce, "I come from your friend Gestes Demias. He wants me to conduct you to the dungeon where he is held."

CHAPTER XVI

On the Jerusalem Road

1

I soon learned what transpired after Gestes handed me Lais' letter and limped away, wounded in heart as well as body. He left Bethpage and made his way back along the Jerusalem road until he came to a partially tumbled-down rock fence. A cold evening wind having set in, he crouched behind the ruins for shelter and gave himself up to bitter meditations.

Protected from the elements, he had been lying there for an hour or more when two shabbily dressed Hebrews rode up on asses and, after looking carefully about, lifted four heavy bags from off their mounts and hid them among the fallen rocks.

Surprised and somewhat frightened by this intrusion, Gestes took refuge behind a large boulder to evade detection. From this position, he watched the newcomers as they completed their maneuver, made their choice of a windbreak and settled down behind it. He might then have lost interest in the pair had it not been for the particular subject of their conversation.

They were, he gathered from their discourse, Jerusalem moneylenders in disguise. They had come with bags of jewels and gold to await the arrival of a desert chieftain, a Zealot, who was to conduct an insurrection in the hope of overthrowing all Roman authority in Judea and crowning Jeshu 'King of the Jews.'

Overhearing these plans, Gestes lost his reason. Springing to his feet with a heavy stone in each hand, he charged the disconcerted Hebrews, and almost before he knew what had happened, he killed them both. Only when he saw the two men lying lifeless upon the sand, did Gestes come to realize the magnitude of his crime.

He looked fearfully about to see if anyone had witnessed the murders. No one was in sight. He started on the run for Bethpage but had covered only a few paces when a thought brought him to a sudden stop: the merchants' valuables! Raised to further the career of a religious zealot, how fittingly ironic it would be to use the gold to advance the work of a zealous anti-religionist!

He surveyed the landscape for possible observers. Aside from the merchants' two fleeing asses—they had taken fright and bolted when their masters were attacked—he could see nothing moving upon the moonlit horizon. Finding no cause for immediate flight, he hurried back, took up the bags one by one, and hid them in a limestone pocket beneath a mound of rocks.

He then started once more for Bethpage, walking as fast as his throbbing wound would permit.

2

Gestes was still some distance from Bethany when he heard the thudding of distant hooves and turned to see a horseman bearing down upon him at full speed. Forgetting his wound he started to run.

Without looking back he could hear the rider fast overtaking him, but he hoped to reach the outskirts of the village and escape the horseman among the houses and olive groves. He succeeded in reaching the outermost buildings when he was ridden down in the dusty street.

Badly bruised but still conscious, he managed to conceal himself in the lower branches of an ancient olive tree.

The chieftain dismounted, drew his sword, and came after him. Gestes clambered from the tree, dropped to his feet on the far side, and won the ensuing race to a nearby cottage.

Aroused from their sleep by the commotion outside their house, a man and his two sons appeared armed with scythes. Others came running from neighboring dwellings.

The two combatants were captured and held, each of them bringing loud and still louder charges against the other.

"Insurgent!" Gestes cried.

"Murderer!" the chieftain bellowed.

Unfortunately for Gestes, the charge of "insurgent" was synonymous with "patriot, deliverer," or some such supreme honor among his Hebrew captors. "Murderer," however, meant one or more of their countrymen had been foully slain.

Gestes was held in Bethpage until morning and then taken to Jerusalem. Not being a Roman citizen, he could not demand a trial in Rome but had to submit to one in Judea before Hebrew authorities.

His story of insurrection fell upon biased ears. He had only his word to prove it, and this of course was deemed no proof whatsoever. The desert chieftain was no chieftain at all, according to his own testimony, but merely a passerby who had accidentally stumbled upon the corpses of two Jews and, seeing the murderer fleeing, had ridden him down out of a sense of civic duty.

Since Gestes' victims proved to be two of the most influential merchants in all Palestine, his destruction would have been a foregone conclusion had it not been for the fact that Jewish authorities were not permitted to sentence someone to death without first obtaining permission to do so from the procurator. It was generally known that plots against Rome were promoted throughout Judea, and Gestes knew he had a good chance of freeing himself with his story of insurrection once he was taken before a Roman magistrate. His captors also saw the possibilities in this direction and acted accordingly.

Knowing Pontius Pilate was busy with other affairs during the Passover feast, they sought and somehow succeeded in securing his decree without producing their prisoner. All was lost!

After that, Gestes was able to prolong his life, for the rest of the day at any rate, only by persistently maintaining he knew nothing of the merchants' treasures. It was not until he was handed over to the Romans that night that he succeeded in getting someone to come to me with a message.

CHAPTER XVII

The Nemesis

1

Gestes was still telling me about his crime, capture, and conviction, when a messenger arrived to notify us that Jeshu had been condemned and, to ridicule his claim to being "King of the Jews," another malefactor was to die on one side of him and Gestes on the other.

Even this humiliation could not shake Gestes' mental equilibrium. He calmly heard the messenger's story, then turned to me, smiled wanly, and said, "I wonder whether the future worshipers of Jeshu will choose to picture me as an elephant or as a lamb?"

To my questioning look, he responded, "You evidently have never heard of the old Celtic Druid god, Hesus. He was crucified with an elephant, symbolic of the enormous sins of the world, on one side of him, and a lamb, symbolic of the minuteness of man's innocence, on the other. What pessimists these atoning saviors are! What cynics!"

After a brief silence in which I tried desperately but in vain to find something appropriate to say, Gestes continued: "You know, Servilius, the dramatists of my country, especially Sophocles, often noticed that a relentless fate pursues certain mortals and changes their destinies. Even before the dramatist, this force, as personified in the Olympian named Nemesis, played a great part in the world's religions, arts, and general history. And have you not observed how like Grecian Fate this Nazarene has hounded me the last few years?

"He destroyed my swine, indirectly brought about my discharge by Marcus Numba, was instrumental in my coming to Jerusalem, thwarted my scheme in the Temple court, lured Lais away from me, caused me to lose my reason and kill two men whom I had never seen before, and now would add to the shamefulness of my death.

"Did they but know these things, I have no doubt that his followers, if he still has any in his adversity, would read grave counsels into my life's story. Tell me, my introspective friend, just what do you make of it all?"

I hesitated, uncertain what to say or what manner in which to say it. His mention of the Fates caused me to wonder if possibly some of his lifelong self sufficiency was not failing him, if perchance he was not casting about for an element of mysticism to draw upon in his impending agony. At last, but with considerable misgivings, I said, "If I were the least bit religious, I would probably say you were punished by the true gods for not having killed a false one that day in Galilee, the day after Jeshu drowned your hogs. Being unable to offer this solution in good conscience, I must admit I have none."

My fears were immediately alleviated. "Good!" said Gestes. "I'm glad to know I have converted someone to my doubts, attitudes, and opinions. It offers me my only hope of a life after death. "Good," he repeated after a short pause in which he seemed to be collecting his thoughts. "To think at such an opportune time, I should obtain from you such a consoling admission…

"Men," he said, turning to the guards with a rather shocking impatience. "I'm ready when you are."

"But," objected an elderly jailer who had visited Gestes periodically through the past night in an effort to win him over to Mithraism, "please my son, before you go, won't you eat this little pinch of wheat bread and drink this little drop of wine I have so hopefully prepared for you? Don't be hard of heart, please. You're such a handsome and intelligent youth. God has given you so much to be thankful for, and it is such a horrible death to which they are dragging you. Please son, in partaking of these, the flesh and blood of our beloved savior Mithra, you will rob this earthly death of its heart-rending bitterness by taking unto your mortal body some portion of divinity. It will be such a comfort to you in your suffering. In commemoration of the Savior's last supper, we…"

"Yes, yes," interrupted Gestes, gently patting the old man on his stopped shoulders. "I know all about your custom of theophagy or god eating, Father. I have had occasion in the past to trace it from its probable origin—the belief among savage and semi-savage peoples that by eating of a dead body they gained the qualities of the deceased: the strength or courage of a lion, the cunning or swiftness of a fox, or the wisdom of a dead chieftain—to its present, supposedly exalted, form: the doctrine that by consuming the flesh and blood of a god one acquires 'some portion of divinity.' Even this simpleton who is causing my death has often said, in his role of the Jewish Messiah, "Except you eat the flesh of the Son of Man, and drink his blood you have no life in you. But, who so does eat my flesh and drink my blood, has eternal life; and I will raise him up at the last day.'

"You mean well, Father, and I am not unappreciative of your concern. If it were just between the two of us, I'd gladly do this thing purely for the satisfaction it would give you. Yes, even though it is just such kind-hearted old devils as you, men who would be princes in any garb and devotees of any doctrine, who do incalculable evil by bringing sensible people to believe there must be some worth, beauty, and solace peculiar to religion."

He paused for an instant, and I could see by the hardening of his face, with what grim resolution he was striving to beat down unwanted emotion. He was only partly successful. When he spoke again, it was with increasing bitterness. "As for me, I always see behind the beauties of a childish faith the grinning satyr of self-deception. If it is a fact, and I don't believe it is, that one possessed of such faith lives happier and dies less grievously than a skeptic, it carries no more weight with me than the fact that a drunk is more hilarious than a sage. In the final reckoning such happiness, it seems to me, is of a contemptible and subservient quality. For although fancies may prove more attractive, enduring satisfaction may be won only by adapting our lives to reality.

"In Athens, I once met a man who claimed and, I have no doubt, conscientiously believed he was a reincarnation of Alexander the Great. He was probably happier for his belief. Just so, this Jeshu of Nazareth believes himself the Son of God and is probably happier for so believing. But despite their happiness, I have no envy of such lives, and I certainly would not advocate that others adopt their manias.

"Furthermore, I have seen entirely too much suffering resulting from an indiscriminate kindness of heart and goodness of intent to concede them any unconditional praise. The evils done by kind and good men often outweigh those done by villains. I am going to the cross because of a good man's wrongs or stupidities—in their consequences, the two are the same. He, idealistic menace that he is, would have men 'resist it not, but return good for evil.' Although far less fanciful, how much wiser, more practical and humane is the attitude of Confucius: 'Recompense injury with justice, and recompense kindness with kindness.' Unless a man has the saving merits of knowledge and judgment, it is as dangerous for him actively to attempt good works as attempt bad ones. Maybe more so, for badness at least has this to its credit: it tends to bring about the destruction of the bad. On the other hand, as sadly paradoxical as it may be, a blind exercise of kindness, sympathy, forgiveness, mercy, and other such leniencies invariably breeds their opposites by preserving the exponents of these opposites. Any good carried to excess defeats itself. I believe it would not be an exaggeration to say one-fifth of all human misery is a direct outcome of misdirected kindness. I am certain the one greatest mistake the world has ever made or ever will make is its placing love above intelligence. Goodness and kindness are virtues in the sagacious; in the undiscerning, along with every other drive to action, they are vices.

"Should I assume your savior to be the co-author of this world, as you do, Father, I could no more bring myself to hold Him benevolent and just than malevolent and unjust. If man needs a god at all, he needs two: an evil and a good one; one to blame for his misfortunes, one to thank for his blessings; one to curse in his wrath, and one to venerate in his rapture. When, as I do now, a man finds himself the victim of perverse circumstances, and is denied a chance to act, he can gain an emotional relief in either of two ways. He can pray or he can curse. Of the two, almost without exception, I believe it is better to curse. It accomplishes the desired end, and it neither obscures the nature of the wrong, the cause of its happening, nor the method, if such there is, by which it should be corrected. Wrongs left to God are never righted.

"Personally, until my energies ebb so low that I no longer can, I intend to curse the good-intentioned but evil-working human jackass who brought about my ruin. After that, if for the first time in my life I feel the need of a god—and I don't believe I will—I know some hundreds or even thousands, one as good as the other, from whom to choose.

"No, Father, with all due thanks for your motives, I must refuse your sacrament. To me, under the present conditions, it would be the bitterest of bitter poisons."

2

As we left the dungeon and made our way across the city to join the Nazarene, Gestes, having found his Roman guards could not understand Aramaic, spoke to me in that dialect. "Needless to say, Servilius, this is far from the manner in which I would like to have ended my days. One finds so much to do and say once he realizes there is no longer time left for doing and saying. I feel I am leaving so much undone I could and would have accomplished, so much the world so much needs. Only one thing is now left to me. In my works, I believe I have amassed such a bulk of data as will convince any sensible man of the falsity of all known religions in which there is any element of anthropomorphic supernaturalism; in my life, I believe I have convinced those who have known me that these religions are unadvisable; and, in my death, I believe you and I will find it wholly unnecessary to hold any religious convictions whatsoever in order to die, even on the cross, without loss of courage, dignity, or self-reliance.

"As you know, I have in Tiberias several manuscripts, some of my own, some of my father's. I hate exceedingly to suspect no special good will ever be derived from these works. Always hoping to some day, somehow, secure the money I felt necessary to launch them properly, I have unwisely delayed getting these books copied and on the market. Now I never shall.

"Some of these writings are as complete as they can be to accomplish the specific ends for which they were intended.

Others of them are not. If you are at all embarrassed by the proposition, pretend now you wouldn't so much as consider such a thing, but once I am dead, take these writings for your own. Study those that are complete until you have made them your own and, drawing from them, try to finish the others. If properly handled, I believe they will be a source of considerable pleasure to you. Just as a man can be damned by faint praise, just so can he be exalted by excessive damnation. This has long appealed to me. After due consideration, it probably will to you. As for taking what was really mine, you can in no wise injure the dead."

This realization caused him to pause for a second, a second in which I tried desperately to think what to say. Before I could say anything, he continued: "I have with me a map I made before you arrived this morning. Together with a few verbal directions I will give you later, it will lead you to the treasure I hid the night before last.

"Don't be in too big a hurry. I believe there was a considerable sum in those bags. The place will undoubtedly be watched quite closely for some time. Wait until you consider it safe to do so, then dig up this money.

"Lais is young, and sex in her kind is not easily perverted. Should she be so fortunate to live down this messiah mania, you will recall how much I cared for her, and do what you can to ensure her happiness.

"Resign from the legion, take this treasure, and go to Rome. There, such books as yours will be appreciated—by some few at least. You will find in these works, as in the Socratic dialogues, many more questions than answers. I have studied fully as much to vindicate my doubts as to validate my convictions. For this reason, I readily and unblushingly admit, my writings are largely, although by no means wholly, iconoclastic. Yet I have not made so much an avowal of my own skepticism as an expos of the puerile credulity of others. It is much more difficult to discover truths than errors, and when I could not grasp the fact, I did the fallacy. To recognize certain mysteries as unsolved, if not unsolvable, and to condition one's life accordingly, has ever seemed to me one of the greater parts of wisdom. He is no thinker who is not willing to follow evidence wherever it may lead, whether to affirmation, or negation.

"The man who refuses to see a thing when it is within his power to see it, I hold to be a liar of the most contemptible variety. With me, when unable to do more, it has proved sufficient, and no small sufficiency at that, to convert numerous mistaken 'truths' into unmistakable fabrications. Next to the man who discovers a new fact, I esteem the one who demolishes an ancient error. Witlings have long bared their fangs at those who 'tear down a thing without putting something in its place.' If you find a scorpion in your bed don't throw him out until you can put a beautiful maiden in his stead. What rot! With what better could one replace many of our so-popular imbecilities than with their absence? What but with an open-minded, critical, and persistent determination to know actualities for what they are can we utilize reality for all it is worth in bettering our almost infinite potential lot upon this earth?

"For much too long now have we listened to admonitions to be humble and supplicating, to accept and conform. Each new generation has been held duty-bound to a servile respect for the preceding generation, its customs, authorities, and traditions, with the result that humanity has grown stagnant. Each year that we have withdrawn from Democritus has, so to speak, put us just that far prior to his time, just that far prior to the dispensing of intelligence. The day is long overdue when we should begin to encourage doubts, investigations, and forward-moving steps. It is in his future possibilities far more than in his past accomplishments that man can claim himself a superior being.

"If by atheism is meant a positive belief in the nonexistence of a deity, then I am not an atheist. For all I know to the contrary, there may be innumerable deities and even deities of deities. Like Protagoras: 'Concerning the gods, I cannot say whether they exist or not.' With Xenophanes: 'There never has been and never will be a man who has certain knowledge about the gods. Even if he should happen to speak the whole truth, yet he himself does not know it... Mortals fancy gods are born, wear clothes, and have voice and form like themselves... Yet if oxen and lions had hands, could paint and fashion images as men do, they would make the pictures and images of their gods in their own likeness; oxen would make them like oxen, lions like lions.'

"All I can say is this: I have never found anything indicative of an intelligent interference in, or governance of, natural forces such as I believe we could expect from a god; I have never run across a theory of the relationship of the infinite to the finite that has not seemed to me palpably absurd; I have never found ample proof of his existence to justify an endorsement of any anthropomorphic deity of whom I have ever heard; and, as for calling a non-anthropomorphic power or force by such capitalized names as God, the Most High, the Almighty, or the Creator, I am of the opinion this but leads to misconceptions, evasions, and other such evils. I would hardly advocate the lenience of Lucretius:

> 'Whoso desires to call the ocean Neptune,
> The grain-crop Ceres, and prefers to abuse
> The name of Bacchus rather than pronounce
> The liquor's proper designation, him

> Let us permit to go on calling earth
> 'Mother of gods,' if only he will spare
> To taint his soul with foul religion.'

"Best avoid such practices all together. I cannot accept the unknown as proof of anything saving of course, my lack of information. Where there is a reasonable doubt, it seems to me ill-advised to be positive. To hold, as practically all religions do until definitely disproved—and there are those who would gladly see anyone killed for even attempting this disproof—that what has been handed down to us for truth must be revered as truth; that acceptance is the ultimate in learning; and that the many gaps in man's knowledge which cannot yet be filled in with facts must be bridged over by faith; to hold these views is but to enshrine Ignorance as the Goddess of Wisdom.

"Some things, since they appear to be true, or at least of worth, I admit into my storehouse of information for daily use under such labels as Sentiments or Suspicions. Some of these are among my most prized possessions. But my outlay of Certainties is very meager, and my estimate of them is not great.

"There are, however, some few items in this latter category by which I swear: so long as acceptance is held indispensable to salvation, inquiry will be futile, if not fatal. There is no shutter for an open mind like religion. We need less faith in the supernatural and more in the courage and intelligence of human beings. Man, once he ceases to rely upon Heaven's aid, will find an unprecedented happiness in what he can create using his own faculties. The Greeks of some four or five centuries ago, finding their faith in the gods destroyed by reason, for salvation turned with unexampled bravery to their own minds and worked out rational systems by which they lived the most complete, the most creative, and the most beautiful of all lives yet known to history.

"There was a time when religion with its grotesque metaphysics, human sacrifices, phallic orgies, prayerful begging, theurgy, and goety had its place. This was man's first effort to control his environment; it was the best tool he knew himself to possess. With the rise of Greek philosophy and its culmination in Democritus, supernaturalism was, or by all means should have been, relegated to the questioned, if not the outworn. If the Abderite and his predecessors did not answer any of the many basic questions man asks about Final Causes, the Ultimate, and the Unknown, they at least showed the religionist's answers to be both untenable and inadvisable. Throw one upon his own responses, and he will learn to use them properly. Let man but realize the universe is indifferent to his wants or needs, that he alone is responsible for his destiny, and he will make that destiny far more resplendent than ever Heaven will.

"No, I am by no means solely and certainly not sentimentally an iconoclast. I have always preferred to prove rather than to disprove. To reject anything as wrong without due reason for doing so is itself wrong. Blind skepticism, like blind credulity, is stupid."

Gestes fell momentarily silent, lost in thought. Then, as if suddenly remembering he was not alone, he said to me, "You will not, of course, allow possession to cause you to overestimate the value of these books. There are many questions they don't even ask and still more they don't answer. They will not live forever, and you will not live because of them. The only books that last from century to century are those like Homer's, Sophocles' and Virgil's: those which offer man a flattering, soothing, and greatly sublimated picture of himself; those which close the gates of cowardly minds against their own pettiness and against the stern realities of life and nature."

Once again he seemed to be drifting. Half to himself he said, "What a picture it would make: *An Idealist Brought to Bay by Facts*. What a lesson in literary criticism it affords!"

I brought him back by asking, "What critics should I attend to?"

"Read them all. Here in Jerusalem you can purchase the writings of Plato, that manipulator, that lover of knowledge who would have constructed a utopian state upon a foundation of religious and political duplicity. Afraid to face realities, he took refuge in ideals. You will have little trouble in finding his books. Why? Because he gives us a most delightful picture of what man likes to consider himself to be.

"But try to locate a single scroll by the venerable sage of Abdera, with one possible exception the world's foremost human source of wisdom, the last thinker even among Greek philosophers who sought for the truth without an ulterior motive. More than half of Plato's common sense, Democritus originated; all Plato's nonsense, Democritus refuted. Yet you can find Plato anywhere, while the Abderite, despite his being one of the two greatest prose stylists in Greek literature, is fast being relegated to oblivion. He is too wise and too honest, both with himself and with others, to live in the minds of men.

"Many will despise your books for much the same reason they despise those of Democritus. You will enjoy to the fullest such praise as they bring and profit by what rational criticism they inspire. But above all you will bear in mind most of the adverse comments they raise will be only the vomit of little minds unable to stomach such heavy disillusionment.

"I have a grave mistrust of systems, and yet I recognize the necessity for them. It is a sad but notable fact that the human mind glories in building dungeons for itself; yes, or sepulchers. I have only contempt for the man who has his system of values handed down to him and is a slave to that system. I greatly admire the person who builds up his system of values and remains bigger than it is. As I once stated, men turn to religion because they want one answer to all questions: 'God'. In a similar manner they too often turn to the various systematic philosophies, Platonism, Aristotelianism, Stoicism, or Epicureanism to get not one answer, but one type of answer. A man entrenched in a system is unable to apprehend contradictory realities. Ready-made moral or philosophical axioms are less often voiced by those striving to acquire a discriminative ability than by those in whom this strife has long since ceased to germinate. Bear in mind, however, it is much easier for a man to act a part than for him to originate one, much easier to follow a formula than to exercise judgment, and I believe you'll find a scholarly bearing is less often evidence of brains than a substitute for them.

"My father was of the opinion that the seat of religion was a special sense of sacredness which has somehow found its way into the human breed. He believed a man is either born with or without this sixth sense: if with it, almost nothing can deprive him of it; if without it, almost nothing can impose one on him. The most that can be done by educating either of these men is to make him tolerant of the other; the most that can be done by bringing pressure to bear upon either of them is to make of him an acting hypocrite. Mindful of a passage in the poetry of Theognis of Megara over which he often pondered, a passage which runs: 'We look for rams and asses and stallions of good stock, and we believe good will come from good; yet a good man minds not to wed the evil daughter of an evil sire... Marvel not the stock of our folk is tarnished, for the good is mingled with the base.' My father was all for trying to breed this sixth and degenerate sense out of the human race. He would have those who are born without that which he saw as a mark of mental inferiority strive to insure the triumph of his own kind. Yes, even if he has to resort to the same measures the religious do to silence, dominate, or kill off the non-religious.

"He believed toleration, if indulged indiscriminately, is less apt to prove a virtue than a vice; that it is one of the first duties of any rational man to determine when and where not to exercise lenience. It is to those who have known what not to forgive and forget that we owe practically every advance we have made away from the barbarian, even those seemingly contradictory advances we have made toward cooperation, companionship, human kindness, and common decency.

"He would have allowed a man his gods, if he was unfortunate enough to have been born in need of them, but he would have made him keep his puppets to himself, not try to install them as despots over other."

Gestes, at this point, again fell silent. Thinking that he might be going back over what he had just said to determine whether or not to qualify any of it, I left him to his deliberations. But when—after a lapse of what seemed almost hours—he remained silent, I feared he was thinking about his crucifixion, so I began to cast about for something diverting to say. Recalling his last assertion, I made this somewhat puerile concession: "That is all well and good, Demias, but what of the men—and there are thousands of them—who are unable to realize these things? What of the man who is born incompetent to build his own ethic, to create and govern his own gods? What solace do you offer him?"

"Very, very little," said Gestes. "Nor would I offer him more. Before I would see extended to anyone the privileges and honors due a member of the race which produced such men as Democritus, Hippias, Hippocrates, Epicurus, and Lucretius, I would see it demanded he possess at least some of the characteristics exemplified by them. I would see the cream of things go, not to the most, but to the best.

"Take that old woman who bought salve from us the other day for her blind child. What solace could I offer her? What real solace can any power known to man offer her?

"Tell her all men are equals in the sight of God. Tell her to seek first the Kingdom of Heaven and all things else will be given her. Tell her: 'Blessed are they that mourn for they shall be comforted.' Tell her to forgive her enemies and bless those who persecute her, that all vengeance belongs to God. Tell her to ask and she shall receive, that faith moves mountains! Tell her God is in His Heaven and will see that all things come out for the best in the end!

"Such things are all right to tell men with faith, but what are you going to tell those with brains? What are you going to tell the man who realizes the mountains moved by religious faith bar the path of human progress? That the price of seeking the Kingdom of Heaven is to inhabit the kingdom of fools? That to put one's trust in the superhuman is to degenerate into the subhuman? That, in short, the fruits of a belief in an after-life is the loss of the fruits of the present life?

"To allow man the hope of a better world after death is to minimize his efforts to better this one, for as the Nazarene well said: 'Where your treasure is, there will your heart be also.' Allow man to believe God will right his wrongs, and he ceases to right them himself. Let him believe he can gain a thing by prayer, and he ceases to work for it. Let him view life as a vale of tears, and he will make it one. Allow him to believe God reveals things to him, and he becomes so completely and finally certain that he not only stagnates, but he demands the stagnation of others as well.

"Perhaps my most stringent objection to faith is that it gives the witling a sense of certitude which a man of critical judgment cannot possibly maintain. If one is but sufficiently uninformed, he knows everything. Religion sustains that element of humanity which is overripe for destruction; it champions the cause of those whom the progress of civilization has left in the lurch; it makes those who are least worthy to propagate their kind the most prolific. The less intellect they have, the more children of 'God' they beget. By maintaining life in such multitudes of the idiotic and depraved, it gives existence itself a sordid and hopeless aspect. Convince these simpletons of the falsity of their energizing beliefs, and if they didn't perish through a lack of motive for living, they would at least be made the more subject to elimination by other causes.

"Together with my father, I am convinced it would prove one of the longest steps in humanity's uphill climb, a climb which, above all things else, makes life worthwhile to thinking human beings, should the sagacious become as actively intolerant of idiocy as are the doltish of intelligence. Any lover of truth who finds knowledge degraded or denied by any faction whatsoever must oppose that faction or be false to himself. As it is now, the dull use all their resources against the wise (it was not by accident the Hebrew scripture writers made the father of knowledge a serpent, despised, distrustful, and poisonous), whereas the learned idealize their failure to retaliate in kind. It is an unequal fight, ever has been and is fast becoming more and more so. We can already detect the unmistakable forecasts of a calamitous end if it is continued much longer on its present basis.

"For two or three hundred years now, a rising tide of undisguised and uncompromising hostility to enlightenment has been sweeping over the world. Countless religions, the worst type of religions—they are almost without an exception, evangelistic, absolutist, idealistic, and above all intolerant—are struggling for the domination of the Empire. Go where you will, you will find men engaged in the business of the gods. The temples of all cults collect a special tribute for the purpose of sending out these 'fishers of men,' or better, fishers of fish in men's clothing. We see these exponents of the different cults beginning to clash. If something does not stem the tide, it takes no great seer to foretell the eventual coming of a veritable religious carnage, the one most blighting curse to which luckless man has fallen heir.

"It seems almost unbelievable that everywhere I have ever been I have heard it claimed that religion is one of our foremost blessings and our greatest need is more of it. From a lifelong study, and an almost world-wide observation of its workings, I believe we would be much better off with less, a great deal less, than we now have, and best off with none at all. In the whole outlay of human inventions there is not one that has added more to human misery than institutionalized religion.

"It is an almost universal assumption that faith enriches the emotional life, that it is an unmixed solace to the bereaved and an unfailing buoyance in times of trial and distress. Will the facts bear out such an assumption?

"Who, especially if he has mingled with the more active elements of humanity, has not seen a dying man, together with his comrades, to whom the assurance he would soon pass beyond the torments even of God might not have proved as great a solace as ever the promise of Heaven has to others? The prospect of an afterlife is consoling only to those who are positive of reaping a reward. To anyone else it is a horror. It is by no means always those most deserving of a reward who are the most certain of receiving one. Quite the contrary!

"It was an observance of how much more unhappiness than happiness resulted from man's fear of the gods that led the poet Lucretius to join the Epicurean philosophers in rejecting 'foul religion.' Even such joys as religion undoubtedly affords, as I pointed out to you not long ago, are often far from praiseworthy. They are but the delectations of dementia. In my book on religio-sexual phenomena, I have shown that the great elation experienced when 'rejoicing before the Lord,' is frequently a morally disintegrating force, as all irrational excitement is apt to be, and just another form of sexual perversion.

"Whereas not one of the sciences, for the purpose of upholding its ideas, has ever allied itself with civil authority, has ever subjected anyone to any form of persecution, or in any way whatsoever besmirched its records, consult the bloodstained scrolls of ecclesiastical history and you will find the same means have been employed to establish and maintain every widespread theology: war, imprisonment, falsehood, betrayal, cruelty, and crime. I am unaware of a single example of a society dominated by clerical power that has not been stagnant, corrupt, and brutal. Religious and civil progress vary in inverse ratio, the more luxuriant the former, the more stunted the latter.

"Whereas every religion known holds faith an inviolable duty, every science recognizes it as a hindrance, since it is fatal to all those inquisitive and innovating habits which are necessary to intellectual progress. Sacredotage has done more damage to life than any one item in the whole catalog of vices. By bestowing upon it God's blessing, the worst wrong is made a sacred right. Yet, there are those who would hold a religious conscience the only criterion of truth, nobility, and rightfulness.

"Name any crime or any form of degeneracy known to man, and I believe I can cite you a god to whom it is sacred, a religious conscience which sponsors its perpetration. Murder? Are not the Sicarii, dagger bearers, a sect of Judaism, conscience driven to killing Romans for God's sake? Did not the Psalmist say of his captors, the Babylonians: 'Blessed be he who dashes the brains of your little ones against the rocks?' War? 'And *Yahweh* spoke unto Moses saying: 'Vex the Midianites and smite them.' Human sacrifice? Moloch, by no means an uncommon or unpopular deity, is represented as a man with a calf's head, outstretched beseeching arms, and an oven belly with seven compartments, one each for the sacrificial burning of flour, turtle-doves, lambs, rams, calves, bulls and children. During their holocausts, the priests of Moloch, with sistrums and tambours, keep up a weird godly music to stifle the shrieks of the roasting victims. Meanwhile, the other Molochites, men and women, parents, friends and relations of the cooked children, abandon themselves to all manner of religio-sexual rites.

"But, I haven't time to pair off each crime and its sponsoring deity. Nor need I do so. Ecclesiastical history accomplishes the task for me. The senseless deprivations, degeneracies, wastes, suffering and dying due wholly to religion is appalling. (If there ever comes a time when man is truly civilized, there is reason to suspect religion will be reduced to the sole functions of coloring and motivating once-upon-a-time horror tales of superhuman villainy, cruelty, and baseness.) Where else in the whole round of human experience can a man gain less from an appeal to either reason or mercy than upon the altars of a foreign god?

"Could I have injected into that salve the other day, unbeknown to them, a quick, certain, and painless poison, I would have rendered that woman and her child the only truly human, merciful, and commendable service within man's present power. The one greatest good we could do such people would be to prevent their being born. One of the sanest things in all the writings of Plato is his advocacy of the enforced aborting of all children other than those by parents who have been inspected, found fit, and licensed by the state to have children.

"True, if we knew some way to lift these creatures up to a human level, it would be well to do so. But, we don't know how and, without that knowledge, it is only religionists and idealists who would keep them alive, allow them to propagate, and perpetuate their misery. There are worse crimes against life than the taking of it.

"It is against just such short-sighted and short-lived kindness as protects God's children that you, as the author of my books, will endeavor to incite the world to scorn and intolerance. In your future work, try to popularize the writings of Epicurus, the sanest of all Greek thinkers next to Democritus. He shows us that the right study of nature must not arbitrarily propose new laws, but must everywhere base itself upon observed facts. Soon as we abandon the way of observation, we lose all trace of actualities and stray off into the region of idle fancies. To look back upon the history of man, it is easy to see our progress toward a better civilization has been as one with our progress away from emotional evaluations, away from the mystical and religious, and toward a more complete reliance upon our own faculties.

"Strive to correct the immeasurable wrongs done to Hellenic learning by the mystical idiocy of Socrates and Plato. Show men that to accord anything too high a sanction is to stay its development. Show them Hippocrates has revealed the only path whereby they can ever profitably endeavor to attain enduring life, the path of medical and physiological research. Show them the nearest man comes to having an immortal soul is possessing an alphabet, for it is in the written word he gains his closest affiliation with the Universal Reason so dear to the Stoics. In writing lies his everlasting, ever-growing race consciousness, which is the real soul.

"Consecrate your energies on the accomplishment of these things, Servilius, and you will not end your life the way so many of your countrymen are doing these days, for the want of something better to do."

3

A great swelling clamor broke in upon Gestes' talk. He handed me the map he had mentioned earlier and gave me such information as he thought needful to supplement it.

This done, he fell silent, as I like to believe, to re-live in memory some of the hours we enjoyed in happier days.

CHAPTER XVIII

The Greatest Lie Ever Told

1

When we joined the dread aggregation which was hurrying the Nazarene and a Hebrew bucolic out to a small hillock, Gestes silently took his cross from a Nubian laborer who had been drafted into carrying it until he arrived.

Jeshu had been brutally manhandled since I had last seen him that morning. He was already too nearly dead to carry his cross. Great welts stood out upon his back where he had been beaten. Some wit, ridiculing his claim to being "King of the Jews," had crushed down upon his head a crown of thorns. Blood ran down his face and formed stalactites in his beard.

Thankful that I had on my military equipage, I stayed at Gestes' elbow and threatened to crack the skull of every humorous imbecile who tried to taunt him. The rabble about was so noisy that conversation was impossible.

Gestes walked silently, his face to the ground, perhaps, to avoid taking with him to the grave a picture of his fellow humans engaged in the one role in which he most bitterly despised them: that of religious persecutors.

2

A man brought forth hooks for sealing the mouths of the condemned men lest they blaspheme from the cross. The centurion in charge dismissed him, saying: "They cannot hurt either Rome or Caesar, and, other than that, let them blaspheme. Offenses against the gods are the business of the gods."

A group of women approached with a bitter liquid called "wine of mercy," a brew of grape musk and gum of myrrh, which brings on a state of lethargy, thereby lessening the sufferings of the dying men. The Nazarene, because he must suffer for the sins of the world, and the other Jew, probably out of a mistaken ideal of manliness, refused to drink it.

Gestes, being the champion of no false values, was more rational. Knowing he must endure the tortures of recurring asphyxia, intermittent headaches, cramping muscles, lacerated nerves, burning, displacement of the bowels, abrasion of the fork, and semi-dislocation of the vertebrae, drank all the bitter wine he could get down.

3

Witnessing Gestes nailed to a cross (which he would have pointed out was no less a phallic emblem than the spear thrust into his side), I thought surely the Nazarene had dealt his final blow. But No!

Suddenly running from the middle of the crowd that had gathered about to watch the crucifixion, Lais flung herself down at Gestes' feet. She began pounding upon the upright beam with her clenched fists, entreating him to accept Jeshu as his one and only God, as the true Messiah.

I sprang to her side and tried to pull her away. She locked

her arms about the cross and continued her frantic supplication. Blood from Gestes' wound fell in her face and blinded her, choked her even, and still she persisted. The sight so sickened me I could no longer touch her.

Anguished, I looked up to Gestes. Calmly he asked me to let her be. Seeing she still loved him, even in her mania, his face brightened. A great kindness erased the marks of his suffering. As a final act of affection, he turned to the Galilean and said: "Lord, remember me when you come into your Kingdom."

The Nazarene, who just the minute before had been heard to cry out in utter despair: *"Eli, Eli, lama sabachthani?"* That is to say, "My god, why have you forsaken me?" Reassured by this admission of his kingship, he faced Gestes and said, "This day you will be with me in Paradise."

Lais, or rather let me call her by her Jewish name, Mary, for she was no longer the beloved "Lais," princess of all the women I have ever known—Mary turned on her knees and, as if in a trance, clasped her hands in ecstasy, glanced up to me through blood filled eyes and said, "He is saved, Marius Servilius. Even with his last breath he saved himself."

Completely nonplussed, I once more looked up to Gestes. With Lais facing the other way, as best he could, Gestes turned both thumbs down and spat toward the center cross.

THE END

Afterword

by Richard Bastian

When he first started school, Leonard Dugger paid scant attention. Education seemed unimportant in a life filled with hardship. His father was trying to raise three boys and two girls by himself in Sweetwater, Texas, after his wife had succumbed to tuberculosis when my grandfather was eight years old.

Grandfather spent one semester herding sheep and reading everything he could get his hands on. He quickly realized that sheepherding was not for him, and he vowed to find a way to complete his education, which he did and with honors. He attended the University of Arizona, majoring in English and History, and obtained a teaching credential, but he didn't want to teach—he wanted to preach! His dreams of becoming a minister ended after he studied the history of Christianity.

Unable to support the teachings of the church, he undertook its undermining, spending the next twenty to thirty years researching, writing and rewriting *The Man Who Owned the*

Hogs, all the while employed as a sheet metal mechanic for Lockheed Aircraft in Burbank, California.

While attending college, Leonard Dugger met Helen Morosco, wife of playwright Oliver Morosco. They teamed up to write a novel, *The Oracle of Broadway*. Mr. Dugger also wrote several short stories, a Hollywood filmscript, and a book of Western poetry.

Upon retiring from Lockheed, Leonard and his wife, Neva Dugger, moved to the central coast of California and built their own home. They raised irises and, with over two thousand of their own variety, boasted the largest iris garden between Los Angeles and San Francisco.

On August 12, 1992, while preparing *The Man Who Owned the Hogs* for publication, my grandfather died. Once a devout Jehovah's Witness, I had always wondered how the staunch atheist would accept death. Would he, at life's end, cry out for God's forgiveness?

I was at his bedside when he passed away. I wish he could have stayed around to hold *The Man Who Owned the Hogs* in his hands, but I'm pleased to report that he died peacefully and with a smile on his face.

References

Page	Source
21	Samuel II:21
	Genesis XXI:1
	Genesis XXX:22
29	Deuteronomy XIII:6-9
30	St. Matthew X:34-36
	St. Luke XIV:26 and 33
	St. Luke XIX:27
33	St. Matthew X:5
34	St. Matthew XIII:11-13
	St. Matthew XV:24 and 26
	St. Matthew XXII:39
	St. Matthew VII:12
45	Ecclesiastes III:19 and 20
	Ecclesiastes IX:2, 4-6 and 10
	Deuteronomy XIV:21
46	Numbers XXV:16 and 17
	Kings XIX:35
	Deuteronomy XX:13 and 14
	Deuteronomy XXI:10-14
	Numbers XXXI:7-18
47	Genesis XXX:3-4
	Samuel II:4
	Samuel XII:11
49	Genesis XX:18
	Deuteronomy XXIII:1
	Leviticus XXI:20
	Deuteronomy XXV:11-12

Page	Source
49	Genesis I:28
50	Genesis XXXVIII:9-10
	Judges XI:37
	Genesis XXXVIII:13-26
	Genesis XIX:30-38
51	Genesis XVII:10-14
	Genesis XXIV:2 and 3
	Genesis XLVII:29
	Exodus XXXIII:9 and 10
	Exodus XIII:21
	Isaiah XIX:19
	Genesis XXVIII:22
	Genesis XXXV:14
	Deuteronomy XXXII:18
	II Samuel XXIII:3
	Psalms XCV:1
	I Samuel II:2
54	Genesis I:2
56	Genesis I:16 and 17
	Genesis V:1 and 2
	Genesis III:22
60	St. Matthew X:11 and 12
	St. John X:7 and 9
61	I Kings VII:10-50
	I Kings VII:36
62	Exodus XX:5
	II Samuel VI:6-8

Page	Source	Page	Source
62	I Samuel VI:19	119	St. Matthew XXIV:38 and
	Ezekiel XVI:17		XXVI:34
64	St. John II:4	122	St. Luke VI:10
67	Deuteronomy XXIII:18		St. Matthew V:5
71	Hosea I:2		St. Matthew V:4
72	Song of Solomon VII:1-6		St. Luke XVIII and XXIX:30
73	II Samuel XXIV		St. Luke X:21
	I Corinthians XXI:14	123	Psalms CXIX:89
78	Judges XIX	125	St. Mark I:5
	Leviticus XI:6		St. Matthew XVI:28
	Deuteronomy XIV:7		St. Luke XXI:32
	St. Matthew XVIII:3	126	St. John X:30
79	Genesis IX:3		St. John XIV:28
	Deuteronomy XIV:7		St. John V:22
	Exodus XX:5		St. John VIII:15 and 16
	Ezekiel XVIII:20		St. John XII:47
	I Kings XV:2		St. John IX:39
	II Chronicles XI:2 and XIII:2		St. Matthew XXVI:52
	I Samuel XXIV:9		St. Luke XXII:36
	I Samuel XXX:17		St. John XVI:33
	I Samuel XXXI:45		St. Matthew X:34
	II Samuel I:1-10		St. John XIV:27
	II Samuel VI:23 and XXVI:5		St. Luke XII:51
80	II Kings XXIV:8	128	Galatians IV:19
	II Chronicles XXXVI:9		Hebrews XI:1
104	St. Matthew XXI:19	131	Matthew VIII:13 83
106	St. Matthew-XII:1	153	St. Luke XIX:31
107	St. Matthew XII:3-5	160	St. Mark XIV:51 and 52
108	St. Matthew V1:26	168	St. John LIV:54
109	Ecclesiastes III:19	184	Psalms CXXXVII:9
113	St. Matthew XIV:25		Numbers XXV:16 and 17
118	St. Matthew V:5